MOVE
UNDER GROUND

Other books by Nick Mamatas:

The Urban Bizarre (editor)
3000 MPH in Every Direction at Once: Stories and Essays
Northern Gothic: A Novella

MOVE UNDER GROUND

A NOVEL BY NICK MAMATAS

NIGHT SHADE BOOKS
SAN FRANCISCO & PORTLAND

Cover and interior layout and design by Jeremy Lassen

First Edition

ISBN 1-892389-91-6 (Trade Hardcover)
ISBN 1-892389-92-4 (Limited Edition)

Night Shade Books
www.nightshadebooks.com

As with any endeavor, there are many people to credit for *Move Under Ground*, but only I can take the blame.

For inspiration, I'd like to thank Richard Schiff of *The Greenwich Village Gazette* for sending me out to the Northport Historical Society's marathon reading of *Big Sur*, and Derrick Hussey of Hippocampus Press for sponsoring the H. P. Lovecraft Walking Tour of Manhattan. Both were eye-openers. Of course, this book would not exist at all without Joi Brozek. Thanks for coming to California with me and having that jerk annoy you in the bar.

The Strange Horizons Writers Workshop helped me out with my first chapter and proposal, and gave me the encouragement to actually keep going. Thanks to editors Jed Hartman and Mary Anne Mohanraj and workshoppers William Mingin, Ef Deal, Michael Belfiore, Nora M. Mulligan, K. Z. Perry, Amy Sisson, Alex Gurevich, and Sandra McDonald. That's in no particular order by the way.

My own cadre of second readers were also extraordinarily helpful: Kynn Bartlett, Daphne Gottlieb, Lynn Reed, JoAnne Cusick, Catelin Compton, and Lori Reaser, thanks! Ditto on the order.

Double thanks to Chris Bell for the cash infusions and diner runs.

Extra special thanks to Sean Wallace and Jeff VanderMeer for their devious machinations.

Triple thanks for Mandy Himel for putting up with me for several months.

Special extra thanks to William Flachsbart for taking care of that thing with the thing.

Ultra cosmic thanks to Jason Williams, who doesn't publish first novels often, and to Michele Rubin, who doesn't agent them often.

This book is dedicated to my parents Panagiotis and Rena, and to my sister Teddie, because they insisted on it.

Book One

Chapter One

I was in Big Sur hiding from my public when I fi-nally heard from Neal again. He had had problems of his own after the book came out and it started being carried around like a rosary by every scruffy party boy looking for a little cross-country hitchhiking adventure. They'd followed him around like they'd followed me, but Neal drank too deeply of the well at first, making girls left and right as usual, taking a few too many shots to the face, and eating out on the story of our travels maybe one too many times. Those boozy late-night dinners with crazy soulless characters whose jaws clacked like mandibles when they laughed are what got to him in the end, I'm sure. They were hungry for something. Not just the college boys and beautiful young things, but those haggard-looking veterans of Babylon who started shadowing Neal and me on every street corner and at every dawn-draped last call in roadside bars; they all wanted more than a taste of Neal's divine spark, they wanted to extinguish it in their gullets. Neal was the perfect guy for them as he always walked on the edge, ever since the first shiv was held to his throat at reform school when he was a seven-year-old babe with a fat face and shiny teary cheeks. He wanted to eat up the whole world himself like they did, I knew from my adventures on the road with him, but I didn't learn what was eating him 'til I got that letter that drove me to move under ground.

The letters had become more infrequent while I was out on Big Sur living in Larry's little cabin, due to me at first, I thought. I was working on my spontaneous writing, which sounds a bit contradictory but discoveries need to be plumbed, not just noted, and I was turning out roll after roll of pages about the stark black cliffs and how it felt that the world wasn't just shifting under my feet but how I was sure one day I'd end up standing still while the big blue marble just rolled out from under me to leave me hanging over the inky maw of the universe. I didn't take breaks except to pick my way into town every week or ten days to get some supplies: potatoes and beans, some cooking oil, whiskey, chaw, more rolls of paper which came in special just for me thanks to Larry, and stamps and my mail. Letters, only three were from Neal, most from mother and my aunt and one or two from my agent with checks so big I couldn't even cash them but instead had to sell them for a dime on the dollar to the one-eyed shopkeeper at the general store that held my mail for me. By that time I could hardly stand to hear anyone's voice so I never spent more than a few hours in town, just enough to do my errands, get my socks washed by the old unsmiling Chinaman and wolf down some cherry pie with ice cream. Even the great belly laughs of the old-timers who had shuffled up from Los Angeles when the strawberry crops had turned black on the vine grated on me when I heard them now, but those curlicue swirls on Memere's letters were soothing and stainless like the sky. I'd read them as I'd hike back up to the cabin, smoking a great Cuban just to have some light to read by if I didn't get home before dark.

Neal's letters were something else altogether, and he was still something else, too, as the kids say. The first letter was typical Neal, full of big plans to play connect-the-dots between girls and writers. "Oh dearest Jack," he wrote to me, "once you're all settled and have ironed up after your latest crack-up I'll come down from San Fran in Carolyn's father's great old battleship of a car, then drive right back up the coast in reverse through Oregon where the trees hold up the vault of the sky. Then we can tour Vancouver; it's a wet warm pocket of life up in those frozen wastes and I know Carolyn has a friend named Suzette you might like as she is very deep into Spengler...." and he'd spin more and more of his golden grift. I'd read his old letters over and over 'til the ink ran off the wrinkled page but only once got around to writing him back. It was too hard to think, being lost in the words of his letters, but they were the only things that kept the horrible roar of the ocean against the cliffs from overwhelming me. No matter what, I couldn't find the Buddha in the rhythmic crashing of the waves anymore, so instead I drank myself into concrete unconsciousness.

In Neal's second letter, the empty spaces between existence became a bit more clear. He could feel it too, how the world was pulling itself apart somehow, and how some dark dream had begun to ooze into the American cracks. He didn't need to say it; Neal was always best understood between the lines. "Far be it from me to suggest that two old Catholic boys take off their clothes, scramble down the bluffs and toss themselves into the foam just to stain the waves red for a precious heartbeat of a moment all to gain the attention of some Three-Lobed Burning Eye, but even when I'm nestled between Billie's legs taking in her fecund smell, I just feel that we ought to...." he wrote, but I knew he meant something else. He was trying to stitch something together; he had some weird forlorn hope that he could save the world from what we both could feel was lurking in the Outer Deep. Usually, I thought of smiling old Neal catting between wife and girlfriend, grinning and pretending to write, misunderstanding Nietzsche in the most brilliant of ways, but now I could only conceive of him as some blind fly picking his way along highway webbing. I didn't write him a letter back after that. Not at first.

I wrote *at* him though, on my old Clark Nova, the one Bill had sent me from Tangiers along with a cryptic note of his own about the little adding machine spring his family fortune was based on. "It only has one end(ing)" he wrote in his junkie scrawl and drew me a swirl that I couldn't look at for long without blacking out. So I wrote to Neal, and to Bill too, but through my novel, not ever in letter form. I wrote 'til the letters on the keys were stamped in my pink blood, long scrolls of philosophy and gin-stewed sex, and I'd take the rolls out to the bush, kick my way to the rocky cliff and roll my scroll down to the shore like a challenge to that Dark Dreamer waiting for us all out in the Pacific. He didn't blink. I'd roll the paper back up, take it home and add it back to the pile of scrolls along one of the walls of the cabin. The air smelled sour for Big Sur. I imagined the old gang could read the display even in the spiritual night and fog—which me and Neal and Bill and maybe even Larry and Allen had all been swimming through (but just a touch on those two, Larry being too much the businessman and Allen too degraded and attached to sodomy to really hear The Call).

When I ran out of paper, which was often enough because I could hardly get it into town to get more and because Larry was just nonplused at what seemed to be my output and could hardly keep up with my needs, I meditated and spoke the mantra of Kilaya 'til my throat cracked like August bark. It was Kilaya: the three-headed demon with bat wings who was converted to the protection of the dharma by the compassion of a wise old lama on a hilltop not too different from the one I was on, who came to me as a pale redhead with great loose curls of hair like a forest fire. She had an excellent belly laugh for a little thing (her ribs were like a pile of sticks) and she whispered in my ear, "College boy. College boy, you look so kind and decent," and made little whirls in my own dark hair with a finger. I worshipped her for two weeks and fell asleep to her whimpering up against my chest. We didn't even need to build a fire or light one of the old blubber lamps Larry had lying around in the dust of his cabin; her skin glowed like holy lightning. I made her three times a night and forgot all about the winedark waves hammering against the shattered cliff face for a few days at least.

She was a humble girl, like deities should be, and humored me by frying up the salt pork and licking thick sour mash off the side of my bottle hours after I'd spilled some, and she even pretended that I was ready to go back to New York with the three hundred dollars I was saving in the crack between logs in the wall against which I stacked all my scrolls for insulation against the wind. "You could buy a car," she'd say happily, a kicky little roadster and take the direct route back to Neal, who was probably just there waiting for me in Washington Square Park. I called her Marie. Marie smelled of sage and crushed grapes and told me that I wasn't long for the world, but not because I'd be going anywhere. I'd have to go somewhere in order to save the world, she said, then she'd pull me back down onto our little mattress and kiss me so hard it was like swallowing an ocean of her. It was a languid week of attachment. I couldn't so much as leave sight of the cabin for fear that Marie would be gone when I returned, even as she warned me again and again that I'd soon be on the road. It was a test of my strength and I was failing miserably 'til I ran out of liquor and finally had to roll back into town to get supplies.

Neal's third letter was waiting for me. It was a package of a roll of paper like Larry sent me, but this one was covered on both sides with writing, some typewritten, much of it scrawled in lead, pen or blood. Much of it was smeared but I didn't wait to read it. I hiked back up the little dirt path to the cabin on the bluff with the scroll in my hands, the paper tossed over my shoulder and unwinding in the dust I kicked up behind me. It was some brilliant stuff, a melding of past and present and dark future. Bill doing his old William Tell routine in a fit of Mexican madness. Me and him in Denver, trying to throw a party. Some haiku. My haiku. The scroll was my writing, at least forty percent of it, transmitted across the aether, painstakingly copied in blood and cut-up between paragraphs and sentences, buried under Neal's own blabbering about Al-Azif and the mad blind tentacle-bearded spawn of the Dreamer of the Deep who were waiting for their old god, nearly dead, to rise again. This could only mean one thing. I had to get to San Francisco. Neal probably wouldn't even be there, but maybe Larry or some benny-addled homosexual would have seen him on the streets, shivering with DTs like a dowsing rod close to a salty marsh and headed somewhere where I could find him.

I tore up to the cabin and threw Neal's roll into the fire where it went up in a belch of black slime and smoke. Marie was there sitting in a full lotus, back arced and humble little breasts presented for me, but I couldn't even bring myself to turn to her. If I did, I'd succumb to attachment. I went to my own wall of scrolls and started taking it apart to get the cash I'd hidden in the cracks of the cabin wall, but found only green and brown shreds of the stuff, wet pulp and rat droppings. I swallowed the curse because bodhisattva was watching and managed to calmly worm a few tired bills, the ones just nibbled a bit, out of the wall. Seventeen dollars. I'd gone further on less, and I grabbed a random scroll for New York to slice into domesticated pages; they could wire the money to Larry for me while I hunted for Neal. Marie transformed into a honeybee, and buzzed a sutra into my ear as I packed my little rucksack. We left together out the door, she hovering about my collar, whispering wisdom and secret knowledge directly to my brain. I didn't even lock up the cabin behind me. The bee once named Marie, also the bodhisattva Kilaya, zigzagged off in every direction at once.

The day was hot and I was slick with sweat even before I got to the highway. Blisters formed and burst on my soles, then the wounds swirled with my salty perspiration. It was only a mile and a half to the road, but I had been lazy with fat sex and ambrosia for nearly ten days, and played a haggard beatnik bank clerk chained to my typewriter for the month prior, so it was a harder stroll than I remembered. The woods were against me too. A canopy of leaves collapsed into a ditch here, a root grabbed my ankle and set me flying like a jiujitsu move from a Navy buddy there. I came across a squirrel drowned in a stagnant puddle, and it looked at me like only a wetsack rodent carcass could. *Don't screw this one up* its black pebble eye said to me, and when you can stare a dead squirrel in the eye and hear it demand a promise from you while even the mosquitoes hover in the air and wait for your answer, you know you got some serious headaches ahead.

The highway was white and near-deserted. Big Sur had become a bit of what some tin-eared newspaperman would call a Mecca for kids looking for real live Beats and the orgies and nitrous parties that were always supposed to swirl up from the rot in our wake, but that didn't last long. Once the newspapermen got wind of it and sectioned our little land off to sell to the public, the tourists came. And after the tourists, the families came in their huge station wagons stuffed with kids screaming for ice cream and white-tile bathrooms and they'd never stop for you, not for one of those crazy beatniks they'd come to see.

Maybe once in a long while you could catch a ride from a lone man. They were the same guys who had souped up their wagons and took to the road at eighty miles an hour, bursting from the wavy horizon just to see how far they could go without even tapping their brakes. Five years later though, their paperbacks were in some attic trunk and old poems ashes and they'd turned to breeding for the goddamn race. No longer could I catch a ride from these mindslave men, though I occasionally caught their eyes as they slowed, tempted as they were to pull over, kick the wife out and load me in for a wild ride up to The City. They were the guys in the short-sleeved button-up shirts, the men with sunglasses pushed up to the tops of their noses, with their arms leaning on the window well of their car doors just to get a little breeze, just so that they could stare into the sun for a moment longer and forget about the mortgage and the PTA and their goddamn uncle-in-law the John Bircher who wanted to set them up fine with a job selling aluminum siding to their own fellow chained oarsmen. But they drove past and turned to their little wives and said "Ah, there's one," and left me to curse on the asphalt.

And it being a hot July afternoon, none of the truckers were ready to stop for me when they could just pull over three miles uproad and guzzle down a gallon of ice water or chilled Cokes along with a pork chop and half a beer, so I put the late-setting sun on my left and started hoofing north on the bloody balls of my feet, thumb out. I walked on, waving my thumb at the empty ghost of a road, occasionally swigging some water from my canteen. It was rough in my bloody boots; now my ankles were chafed as well. I balanced the rucksack on my head to keep the sun off of it, but that didn't help, and the straps had already dug into my shoulders, so I took to swinging it, tossing it 20 yards in front of me, and then leisurely strolling over just to pick the sack up. No wonder I wasn't getting any nibbles from the few folks who did drive by.

It got dark fast; there was hardly any dusk at all. And behind me, I heard the roar of a convoy, but they weren't old trucks coming my way. Instead, it was wagons, sedans, curvy Studebakers, and even a few old crank cars with rumble seats and shivering fabric roofs. Town cars driving five abreast in tight formation across only two lanes of highway, eating up the shoulders, headlights suddenly blazing a terrible, beautiful amber. I cut into the wood and watched them zoom past from a little ditch I happened to fall into. Above the narrow, mud-stained alley I was in, the collective purr of the motorcars choked themselves silent. There were hundreds of cars, it seemed, all stinking of fumes thick enough to cover the scent of the wet leaves I picked out of my teeth and ears. I hustled backwards, lost my rucksack, found it again and fell hard, banging my kneecap like a cymbal. I heard a dozen doors slam behind me, and limped a bit, rucksack in my arm football-style, to put some space and trees between me and whoever that horrible Them was looking for me. The rim of the highway was a ribbon of gleaming off-the-lot paintjobs, even on the oldest cars. Men and a few women, all in their Sunday best including too-hot-for-summertime stoles and those insipid little flowered hats, tromped down into the brush after me, all silent but for crackling branches. Not a "Ho there," or a "Do ya see 'im, Mildred? Do you see the man they say runs the orgies?" and not even an "Ow, I fell into a ditch." Just eerie inexorable marching. I feinted right then veered left, poked under a shield of roots from a tree blown half out of the ground, then cut right again.

And they tumbled after me, a little army of Boris Karloffs and Elsa Lanchesters run through the projector at double speed, herky-jerky, often falling and sliding down a streak of mud, or just wildly but silently smacking branches out of the way on their way down. One man, all white shirt belly and lippy grin was right on top of me, and with a wild but damn quiet leap jumped off the rock he was perched on and sailed over my head. He landed hard enough that my ankles felt it, but without a grunt or so much as a look back at me, he smashed his way deeper into the forest, heading down to the bluffs.

I decided on a little experiment. I stood still, but kept the straps of my little rucksack wrapped around my fist and wrist in case I needed a weapon, and let them come at me. A woman was first—she was huffing like a smoker but was calm-eyed even as she ran up to my chest and smacked into me. She slid off me sweatily with just a half step and kept right on running. She didn't even raise a hand to adjust her little hat, so it fell off and I reached down to snatch it up just to have another little twig of a girl plant a dainty foot on my kidneys and then hop off of me. I grunted hard, but nobody heard or noticed. Then I stood up, wound up my arm and slammed the next fellow I saw right in the side of the face with my sack. I heard the tinny-tin *ting* of my canteen bounce off his chinny chin chin but even this joe didn't turn to face me. He just kept on, his split lip making his smile a lopsided leer, like one of Neal's after a three-day nod. I shouldered my sack, cracked my toes (the poor little piggies were swimming in bloody sweat now), and started easing my way down into the dark of the woods beyond the headlights and ran straight into Dreamland.

It was still woods at first, but woods of a different sort. Cacti were everywhere, scratching me with steel syringes as I passed; then snaking ivy slid over my poor tired boots. I yelped loud and danced away from them, and the rose-red buds opened and hissed at me. The well-dressed gentry nearest my little Mr. Bojangles routine had taken to galloping along on their haunches and knuckles, but a few further away from me were still holding their heads high, like it was time to tell a hotel bellboy what for. They glowed like swamp gas and I could see their faces clearly after I blinked away my sweaty tears. They were hungry. Every one of the souls around me had that hungry fear painted 'cross their faces. The fear of a whore who just lost a tooth and a little bit more of her looks to a pimp slap. Hungry like little Charles Ma filling his opium pipe while sitting crossbones-style up on a palette on the Oakland piers. Not hungry for anything, the way Neal was when I'd met him, when we spoke about writing or when I watched him amble off towards some college girl with knitted stockings and a tucked-up copy of *The Militant* under the crook of her arm, but hungry for nothing. Nothingness. Not even the peaceful touch of Buddha's palm, or the deepest sleep I had on Marie's shoulder just a night ago, but a great big horrible nothing, the nothing that can't stand to be defined by the some things floating around on in it. Then the forest around me, queer as it was already, pulsed and twisted into something else entirely.

The tree in front of me was jelly. I guess jelly, or ectoplasm or liquid aether, a huge pillar of it I'd say, if pillars were made up of slabs of living lard. It wobbled and touched my mind, poking through history and poetry to scoop out the thought-form of lost Terry, the little Mexican girl I made for a few weeks. We had lived in a tent and waited around for her brothers to get me a job collecting manure and selling it to the local cotton farmers, but then I got the itch and headed out on the road again. And now she was there before me. Nipples like brown plums, quiet eyes and little cesarean scars running up her tender belly. For a wrong moment I followed my desire, and her face exploded into a huge gaping Venus flytrap mouth with tentacled teeth. Sweet Jesus, if my boot heel didn't pick that very serendipitous second to split and land me on my derrière, I'd have been meat that night and fertilizer today. But I fell under the snapping and squiggling mouth and kicked hard at Terry's knee. Top-heavy from the snapping head, now atop a whipping stalk of a neck, she fell backwards, but was replaced. A huge wall of Neal's faces, some smiling, some winking, others distracted and even bored rolled up to me. I skittered backwards on my palms, but sweet earth betrayed me, turning warm and viscous then collapsing into a pit. The thought-forms were shambling towards me now, a mass of Neals and Memeres and my poor old brother like he would have looked had he been grown. The coach from damn Columbia and Allen too and stupid Chad and Terry's brother Chavo, and goddamn even Marie with preying mantis limbs as long as she, they were all there surrounding me, with snake bodies or flat snake faces simply plopped atop cockroach legs.

Shapeshifters. The formless given form by thought or evil deed. *Shoggoth.* I knew the word now, somehow, but not from some half-remembered bongo drum poem or off the back of a jar of Ovaltine. Marie-The-Bee had told me on the way out the door, bless her. Stilt-Marie sliced a wandering churchlady in half with a swipe of scythe-arm, and chittered at me, but I couldn't hear her over the splattered meat smacking into what I might as well call the ground. And then I remembered the buzz in my ear from when I left the cabin and the sweet perfume of green grape and sage.

The Master had gathered the students into the courtyard one day and held aloft a butcher's knife, a simple and base act that alone would require a week of ritual cleansing. Worse, then, he drew his other hand from behind his back and held up a cat by the scruff of its neck.

"Stop me," Master said, "from killing this cat. Stop me from performing this base act of barbarism."

The timid semi-circle of saffron-robed students looked up at Master in stunned silence, and with a practiced move, Master lopped off the cat's head. It fell to the ground like an overripe pomegranate. And it came to pass that later a student who had been out gathering alms returned to the temple and, hearing the gossip of the day, confronted his Master.

"And what would you have done?" the Master asked.

The student took off his sandals, placed them on his head, and walked backwards from the room.

Master called after him, "You would have saved the cat!"

So when false Marie dipped her head low into the pit and unhinged her jaw to show me her long tongue with its little face, its little scowling General Eisenhower face, I did the absurd thing and took her cheeks into my hands and rubbed my lips against her hanging horselip. I stroked her wet straw hair and whispered "Oh Marie, sweet sweet Marie," and soulkissed the shoggoth. She melted in my arms. Really. A keening rose up from among the rest of them, and the slick jelly under my feet once again turned to rocky earth. Some retreated, others gave up the ghost entirely and just imploded, sucking themselves into their own pits of dark nothing. Poor Marie sizzled and smoked around me, making my pores tingle. She was trying to gain a more physical *entré*, but I was safe for now. The fog that enveloped me smelled of landfill, and it felt for a long moment that I was in between. Not Dreamland, not old terra firma, just the waking-up-in-the-morning world of blurry shapes and voices. Then the sun pierced the fog, with great holy rays. It was dawn. I was alone again, right at the edge of the bluffs. I felt the ocean on my face.

It took me only a few minutes to scramble down the shore where I found the squares again. They were dead, to a man and woman. Some bashed against the rocks after a great fall, others bobbed in the surf, face-down, bloated and burnt all at once. A few dozen of them there were, maybe a hundred, all in the finest clothing they had, all drifting out to sea or caught up in jaws of stone and muddy sand. I stood out on the jetty and watched a few of the carcasses, fat from tv dinners and Organization Man jobs, float out into the drink. I sat and watched them for a long time while the sun rose behind me and painted the Pacific, red, then gold, then deepest blue. I ate an apple from my rucksack and glanced around, to see if anyone had left behind a purse or a wallet, some identification. I wasn't ready to make like a vulture and pick at these poor souls quite yet.

Hard to notice at first, but the tide was heavier than I expected. Waves pushed up over the rocks, claiming the bodies on the shore. I had to retreat from the jetty and hustle back up the cliff. The waters rose higher than I'd ever seen them, and I looked out to the horizon to see why.

The island was huge, or close, or somehow in a warp of space like a mirage. Miles out to sea but right up against my face in the same instant, I could see the hideous swirls and cut runes on well-worn granite ruins and the whole line of the shore at once. Craggly harbors lined not with boats, but with slick lobster-squid. Thick slabs of stone atop strata of crushed bone, the bedchamber of an Elder God. No gulls circled its beaches, no trees lived there or even stood defiant in petrified death. Even the crumbled doorways had been built for something other than Earthmen. Between me and it, there was only a short boat ride's worth of sea and a trail of white bodies, drifting towards their new dead home.

R'lyeh is risen.

Chapter Two

There was no hideous dreamland between me and the highway anymore, no industrial cacti, nor gearshift branches ratcheting towards me with pincer fingers. Just trees and the bush, still dark after dawn with the stain of hysterical suited mayflies. I put R'lyeh behind me and didn't look back to see if it was still there offshore because, for one, I was afraid that whatever swept up those townspeople would beguile me, and I'd find myself running for the rocks before I even knew what I was doing, and two, because I didn't have to see the shattered island to know that it is risen. I could taste it, like a punch to the face.

I chose the biggest whale of a truck I could find from among the abandoned and spent thirty minutes siphoning more gas from the surrounding vehicles so I could bull out of there with a full tank. The City, yes, San Francisco, I had to get back there and to do that, I rammed through a few dozen idled cars. It was fun, really, and nearly brought a smile to my grim face. Steel against steel, the low roar of my stolen engine (damn, this truck was King Rex in low gear; we put a Packard on its side with a casual nudge), playing the clutch and stick like bop. I didn't look back at the automotive wreckage I left behind either. Let the cops find it, let them go looking for the drivers and find those forlorn bodies in the drink. Let them find the island, closer than Communist Cuba, and call out the Army or the H-Bomb or *Sea Hunt* and gut the Elder God, if they could. I had to find Neal.

I stopped frequently, more frequently than usual. At a rest stop, I fingered the local yokel newspaper. Nothing but wire reports and gardening tips, plus classified ads full of desperate novenas. The shift of the world's axis hadn't reached here yet. The wind was still high, the waitress still slouched and slow and her coffee even slower, the few truckers at the counter still bleary-eyed. Nobody laughed. I asked Millie (she had a horrible plastic tag to that effect, maybe she was really a wisecracker and made up the name to sound authentic) to turn on the radio but she said it blew its tube just before dawn. "It sparked up, and then started smoking. I thought it was Cholly burning the toast at first," she said. Then she launched into some monologue about having to call long distance just to order a vacuum tube because Cholly didn't want to buy a new radio set even though it would be cheaper thanks to some insult that passed between Johnson and Cholly back in '53; it was the sort of thing I'd normally fall in love with but I just wasn't in the mood. Greasy eggs and bacon for me. I broke the yolk with my fork because it resembled an inhuman eye a bit too closely.

I spent an hour nursing a coffee and watching the traffic. All of it was heading south. Me, I rolled north in my dented but still fierce stolen truck after stopping to smear some mud on the plates. The City was farther off than I remembered it, or the old jalopy was slow, or the speedometer a liar or the sun setting too quickly into the Pacific. It was hard for me to travel alone again by car; I'd always preferred the hitch or the bus or a smartly hopped rail. I stopped in a little town just after dusk, one I had never stopped at before. It was called San Santo (Saint Saint? Sounded auspicious, surely. The water tower poking up over the trees off the road simply read SANS from my position).

The one thing the town was not without was alcohol, thankfully. The diner had shut down, as had the store, once it turned dark. I'd never seen corrugated metal gates pulled down over display windows in a town so small. Two stoplights down the main drag, maybe a half-mile square, only the steeple and the water tower topped three stories. Didn't see a school. But bars. Oh the bars, four bars in a *cul-du-sac* waiting for me at the end of this little town. The Tear Drop, The Dead End (they must have really liked their *cul-du-sac*, those two), El Negro for Mexicans and Secrets. I got out of the car and just stood. The aura of beer, just hanging in the cooling air for me to inhale, for free. My body remembered beer, oh yes it did, every pore a little mouth sucking in individual molecules. I was dizzy. Oh, the music. Live accordions from the Mexican joint, and murmured singing punctuated with ecstatic tra-la-las and from Secrets, jazz. A hot five maybe, but with a banjo instead of a piano. From the other two bars, a melody of guffaws and snorting, heavy chortles sprinkled with yelps. Old friends hiding from the deadening night. I wasn't feeling too social though; I could tell from the laughter alone that if I hit The Dead End or walked into The Tear Drop I'd be off the road and settled in for days or weeks of great conversation, fun girls, maybe a job logging or pouring cement with new rawboned buddies who'd thrill to the damn beatness of it all. Tempting, but no. Sans Santo couldn't have me; I needed to get to the City.

I also needed to get to a drink. I had fifteen fifty in my pocket and it paralyzed me. I knew I could get the cheapest booze in El Negro, even if The Dead End looked a bit dingier, but oh the bop. Saxaphone swirling down a whirlpool, the bars of some old standard collapsing into rough chaos I had to go towards it, my eyes off so that my soul could listen more deeply without the distractions of light and shadow. I started walking towards it when I heard a screech squawk and thump. Then nothing but two bright lamps and a silhouette leaning over to comfort the poor chicken that had been crushed under the narrow wheel of the old car.

The Negro cradled the bird in his arms, so warm like Madonna, his skin bronze in the light. And he turned to me and smiled wide, like he knew me. Like he recognized me maybe, from television or the papers. My knees locked and the old fear returned, my stomach dropping into my bowels.

"Peckerwood," he said, still smiling, "Blood's been spilled, so I been called. Take this bird inside. Have 'em cook it up for me. I gotta set." I took the chicken. "You don't mind," he said, nice and slow, but he definitely said, he did not ask. I didn't mind, not once I saw the horn the driver was pulling out of the front side passenger seat of the car. I led them into Secrets, my decision made, and waved the chicken, still alive (one stunted wing fluttered, but its eyes were closed and content) under the bouncer's nose. He nodded economically towards the freckle-faced girl leaning by the kitchen door. She smoothed down her apron when she saw me. I lost the Negro, handed over the bird, found a seat, snatched a cocktail from the table next to mine and blew my mind. The music had stopped; so had the chatter around me. The only thing that was, the only thing in the icy now of San Santo's beerlight section was the Negro. He was slow, head low, practically on the nod, but he was a pillar of his race. The other saxman shuffled off the stage to make way for this man, who stood as upright as a sequoia except for his sleepy, smiling head. He licked his lips. He didn't smile because he wasn't some sort of Satchmo gladhander. He just said "Suite," and played.

Blue and yellow fire belched from his horn. The ground shook like the Big One had finally hit the still far-off City, and something, sweat or blood or even gray brain started dribbling from my ears. It was beautiful; the Negro wasn't even breathing, just blowing, just tying notes in knots, making a tapestry of sound and burning the threads just as quick. Blam! The head to the left of me just exploded, empty lobster exoskeleton and black meat everywhere. The beer boiled away in my mug and I inhaled it like dreamy opium. And the Negro blew some more, terribly, beautifully, in time with the blood swirling in my ears. Another patron, some dude in a dark corner, burst into flame and ran out the door and Negro still blew. Except for the two casualties, the rest of us were really digging the set. He let it die easy, the cornucopia of fireworks sizzling in his horn quietly fading. Blue and yellow to subtler reds and oranges, the key shifting, a downbeat taking over nice and slow like summer.

Then time stopped. No beat, just a low siren whine. Even the light was still, black and color splattered like a Pollock across the bar. But I could move, and I stood up and saw them more clearly. A few sailors (four, one of them without a head, his neck ended in a mass of burnt bone and black meat), a tired older man in a nicely pressed shirt. Beetle mandibles instead of lips stretching from their cheeks. A woman, too, had the mandibles, hers stretched wide open, and she had tentacle fingers wrapped three times around a tall glass. They were frozen, but a few of the other patrons weren't. A good ol' boy poured some horrible booze over the head of one of the sailors and set him aflame. Sort of, he did. It was holy flame, frozen flame, like a cape of phoenix feathers draped over a body due to the timeslip. Flame that didn't crackle or dance, it just was, waiting for the world to start again so it could really eat up the air. The barback pulled a shotgun from under the bar, walked around it and put the barrel of the gun right between the beetle-woman's pincers. And he pulled the trigger. Her head didn't explode, it swelled, then waited. The others were dispatched too by a few of the rougher customers—the whore with her straight razor, some frantic queer in denim overalls with a broken chair leg digging into the chest of another of the squares. The murder was well-practiced, like the local ringers who manage to show up for every game of darts or billiards in bars across the nation. They don't know much, but they know every warp of the felt, or every wayward draft that might push a point into a bull's eye. The folks knew what they were doing, and as the one-note thrum of the sax started slowly turning into the wheedling whine of a siren, I knew that this whole performance had been planned just to draw in and eliminate a few beetlemen and squidhanded girls. The sailor went up like a Roman candle and singed my eyebrows from the across the room. Eyes dazzled, nose filled with beefy smoke, taste of sour ink on the tongue, but in the ears, "Scrapple In The Apple." And then it faded away.

I was alone in the bar, except for the besmocked girl sweeping up a corner full of dust. Three pitchers stood upright, one rested on its side, the handle keeping it from rolling off my little table. I was peering into a knot in a plank of the wall. The freckle-faced girl limped over to me finally, and even her freckles looked mean, but not as mean as her bloody smock. The sun was up, she'd have to close for an hour or so (heck, make it two) to hose down the floor. She thanked me for tipping so well all night, and shooed me outside with slow hula-wave hands and I got to the *cul-du-sac* just in time to see my truck, the truck I'd stolen anyway, drive off with a heap of limbs, torsos, and leaking trash bags in the bed. Easy come, easy go. So I went, into the morning streets of San Santos.

Or should I say street? San Santos was like a town in an old western film, it may as well have been all facades, and a bunch of extras just shuffling around nonsensically in the background. Only the main drag was paved; the side streets were packed dirt, gravel and dried mud. The little diner smelled bland from the open doorway. As weird as the jazz massacre was last night, as insane as the spontaneous mass suicide of two days ago, it was a restaurant full of grown men and women, every single one of them eating oatmeal and sipping water, that was the most unnerving thing I'd seen. I didn't walk out, I backed out, but not one person so much as looked up from their oatmeal. I turned the corner and took one of the rutted footpaths into the downtown area, and oh yes was it down and out. Shacks not only leaning but about to fall over, jury-rigged phone wires low and bowed like clotheslines, a drooling hand pump and not much else in the little square except for life, brilliant sensuous life. A pair of kids whooped it up in a puddle; hobos three of them, two old and a young fellow probably right out of reform school, sharing wisdom in their slurred cant. Girls' hips swayed when they walked here, back down on the mainline, they just tromped like they were wearing summery snowshoes.

I settled in next to the trio once I spotted the bottle they shared. Upstanding already, the young fellow silently passed it to me without even looking to his elders for permission. Chuck was the young guy and Jed and Smitty the older ones (Lord, what names!).

"What's this all about?" I asked. Chuck opened his mouth, but didn't say anything and didn't close it. Smitty ran his fingers over his crackling white stubble. "Well, some people believe," he said, deliberate and slow, like Morse code, "that these are the End Times. But not the very end. The end of one thing, like the town," (he nodded back to the main drag) "and the beginning of something else," (he turned north towards my sweet City) "and the only place left for life is right here. In-between town for in-between people." Then he smiled and showed me his teeth, rotten but pleasant, a natural rot for once. "But it's Jed who has religion, he knows his Revelations. My conceptual framework is more of a Marxist existentialist one; the world's patina of logic and reason is melting away under this summer heat. We're seeing absurdity laid bare."

I looked at Jed; he shrugged and shook his head. So I rapped about Buddha and told them the story of how Kilaya came to me in the form of beautiful woman (Smitty expressed a basic appreciation for that, though the fine point of even the most base of black beings turning towards protection of the dharma was probably lost on a Red, even a half-drunk one) and how a little burst of the absurd had saved me from a shambling horror born of dreams and eldritch force.

"Explain Yardbird then," Chuck piped up. "C'mon Smitty, a damn ghost does three sets a week in this little one-outhouse town, just so the lumpenprole can take out a few bugmen? How does a dialectical materialist conception of history explain that?"

Smitty just flicked a finger against the bottle, making the glass ring like a bell. "Big hominid brains perceive the world in unusual ways, especially under unusual circumstances. That doesn't mean, however, that reality doesn't exist. Why would supernatural beings create a town full of Organization Men? To stuff envelopes?"

A train whistle blew in the distance, bringing me to my feet. "There's a train line here?" I asked. Smitty and Chuck shrugged, Jed spoke. "Evil. It's an evil train."

I just put my hands on my hips and laughed. "Damn, I've seen gods and suicides and ghosts and bug-faced businessmen, all in the past two days, but an evil *train*? Sounds like a pulp story! What makes a train evil?"

"It comes late," Chuck said with a thin-lipped smile. He shared a look with Smitty.

Jed explained: "Evil freight. Evil passengers. San Santo doesn't have four bars because we're drinking inside; they're bars for evil to wet its lips as it passes through our town. Except for Secrets. That's for queens." I clenched my teeth and fists at that. Jed was taunting me or just wanted a punch in the face, which I was just as happy to give him. Something about San Santo was tainting even the tramps; these weren't holy fools, they were flies circling the rot, looking for jack-meat to nibble on. But Smitty told me to relax and that the rail was actually a new line, an industrial and military line for transporting classified who-knows-whats. It's the hobo preachers and hoodoo Negroes who think the line is haunted. He rode the rails just fine though, a number of times, all the way up to Oregon. It's where he met Chuck too, and they were just relaxing in San Santo 'til the old itch returned, then they'd be heading down to Texas to work on some shrimp boats. It was a traveler's invitation—I'm heading this way, taking this route and I'm sure there's enough work and girls and secret pocketfuls of shrimp to cook over open fires or in old tin cans full of salt water for you too. It was a temptation, it was designed to be one. Hollywood-extra scholars of the bottle and paperback philosophy, attempting to distract me from my mission. Even the four bars of San Santo; normally I would have spent four days in this dustbowl, just to get my full of each establishment. It was time to go. I walked off and out of the little camp behind the town, towards the echo of the train whistle.

Whoever slapped San Santo up overnight must have also done the location scouting for the rail line, as it was atop a horrible towering ridge. The locomotive must have looked great as it chugged up the track, slicing the setting sun in half behind it each evening, but laying the rails and keeping the cars from tumbling into the valley I was walking through must have been murder. I had to pull myself up the ridge, kicking footholds in the loose dirt and scrambling for brush and roots as I went. The top of the ridge was just barely wide enough for the tracks, and the ground was cracked where the spikes had been planted. There was only one place to hide on the ridge, an out-of-place boulder just tall enough for a man to curl up behind in the little bit of shade it made, so I walked over, curled up and tried to meditate.

The land around me was strangely empty. I had walked just out of site of San Santo (except for the water tower, which just read TO from this vantage point). The tracks snaked off into a wooded area into the south and up the ridge to a tight turn out of my field of vision to the north.

The other side of the ridge was a valley just like the one I had walked across, *sans* San Santo. The air was too still and even the bugs were having a siesta. I pulled the canteen from my rucksack, set the sack itself up like a pillow held up against the rock by my head, took a swig of warm water and waited for a train or some clouds to roll in from the ocean.

The train was incredibly well appointed. I was waved into a Pullman car with wooden molding, red carpets and wide screened windows to let summer breezes in while keeping grit and flies out. The porter, a smiling shuffling Negro (I was reminded of the Charlie Parker ghost, but this fellow had no soul at all, he was a clockwork black servant) brought me to a little table with a white tablecloth and poured me a tall glass of lemonade from a tin pitcher. We were off, and smoothly. The ridge and the woods rolled past without even a jerk and chug from the car. The lemonade was good but a little tart, like a thimbleful of bitters had been sneaked into the mix. A dessert tray was rolled out: spongy angelfood cake topped with strawberries, dark puddings, an éclair I took; it was surprisingly cool on the teeth. I drank more lemonade, ready for a sour protest after the sugary éclair, but it was just as tasty as the first swallow. There weren't even any chocolate fingerprint stains on my fingers or my canteen; it was still cool on my forehead and the sun had dipped down behind the boulder. It got cold quickly—

Northport's cold at night, especially at the Long Island Railroad train station. The parking lot was empty except for great white lights spotlighting the spaces like a very boring Off-Broadway play just about to start. After the evening commute, after everyone locks themselves up in either their homes or in noisy Gunther's, only the lowly and the lonely hang around the station. Even the stationmaster locks up the waiting room and goes home at 8 p.m. I waited on the platform for a long time, chilly and wrapped up in myself; I leaned against the steel steps leading to the overpass from one track to the other, but the bars were too frigid. A scooter ripped down the street behind me, then across the parking lot, drawing a wild crazy eight of exhaust and teenage whooping. I turned to the east, as if I could see if the train was finally pulling out of Port Jefferson station ten towns away. The gray of the platform was clean, not even a pebble to kick onto the tracks. I waited—

The opportunity presented itself. On the ridge, the train had to take it slow. Out of the corner of my eye I saw car after car and then finally a flatbed. I kept my shoulder to the boulder and spun off of it, ran a great five strides and leaped up, landing expertly between two tarpaulin. Two other riders were nestled in the tarps, one of them toothless and friendly enough to produce a flask instantly. On the edge of the bed, one fellow yelped and staggered as he tried to piss into the wind and got a mouthful of his own juice. But even he walked back to the tarps on wobbly sailor legs and helloed me, his hand wiping and wringing out his beard. Jittery, expansive, like a bag of giggling wind, I felt good to be traveling again—

I snapped to, faded and dreamed again of another train. A spasm, my body shrieking and giggling "TRAIN!" at my mind's tired phantasm, and I woke again to nothing but absence and anticipation. I stretched over the top of the rock like a tired lizard and drifted again, eyes crossed, on the nod. My nerves were all jangled; I needed a calmative, preferably something with a bit more kick than 80 proof. The boulder reminded me of that terrible island, dead Cthulhu stretched and sleeping on black glass slabs, but I was too tired to move. I hadn't slept in days, I remembered, not since I was in Marie's blessed arms. I licked my lips, so dry, and dreamt of locomotives and tunnels. Thirsty, damn thirsty, I wanted to drink civilization. The world flickered into existence now and again, always between dreamland rail stops, always to the excited poking and shaking of goblin Pullman porters.

My canteen was on the ground, empty, the little stain of water in the dirt already mostly evaporated. No train yet, at least I hoped, so I went to the track and put my palm upon it. No vibrations, no real heat, no fresh cracks wrinkling the loose ground around the spikes. I slept through the day (the moon was low and huge like a thumb) but I didn't sleep through the train at least. More waiting, this time walking waiting, up to either end of the ridge. I pissed into San Santo's valley and felt thirsty again. I hoped at least that the hobos I'd meet would be as friendly as the dream forms I'd slept through.

It was light enough to write, but who'd believe it? I could taste San Francisco (salty and sweet, I was getting thirstier). I loved it; I even loved that horrible old job I had, guarding drunken sailors ready to ship out. It was only a few weeks in a shack with a friend and his wife, a few weeks of strolling around with an unloaded gun, of writing up a Hollywood melodrama to be delivered right to Fatty Arbuckle's nephew in exchange for a burlap sack full of gold. I didn't get the gold, of course. I don't even think I got the carbons of the screenplay after the great shack revolt, which ended with me ducking my own typewriter and a shrieking bottle of Jack Daniels and then retreating to North Beach. I could write about that; heck, I did write about it (mostly, with nip and tucks and some work on a smoothing lathe, but as far as the kids knew, I just poured life out onto the page), but R'lyeh isn't the most literate of topics. Hollywood, maybe. Extras dappled with corn syrup blood, writhing and bowing before a giant glowing brain on puppet strings. Tainted pictures for a tainted world.

The train finally came, it *really* finally came and yes it did slow down on the ridge and there was a flat bed covered in tarps and I did leap up on it, but I was alone and cold now. The bed rocked like a ship in high waves as we rattled over the tracks and shot into the woods. I couldn't see what was under the tarp, but whatever it was, was mostly loose and had some give, so I shouldered and nudged my way into a little crevice and made like dead weight.

The trees fell away, and the huge sky was empty and splashed with moon. No clouds, but only three or four stars, bright and wise like Memere. I thought of her, back in New York, clipping coupons and sweeping the floor and petting the kitten. All the bones in my skull rattled; I cupped my hands up to my ears to protect them (my ears, my poor knuckles were on their own) from the whipping wind, so I could hear myself think. Why was I out here, why was I looking for Neal? I couldn't even figure it out why I wanted to go to Frisco, except that there would be alcohol there. I never should have left my poor mother again, I should have stayed on my couch and let those dharma bums come rapping on my bay windows while I was mixing some mayonnaise in my tuna fish. No, not even that. I should have gotten a job: I could teach school, coach some football maybe, or get a desk job with Farrar, Strauss and Giroux. Not a wanderer, but a commuter, that's what I should have been. Northport at 6:36 a.m. with the others, in their trenchcoats and hats, blowing on steaming deli coffee so they—so we—could sip without screaming. I'd stand all the way to Jamaica Station, then finally settle into a seat and snooze 'til we rolled into Penn Station. Then up the escalators, across a bunch of crowded scary streets, with newspaper vendors and doughnut men all for me, then workworkworkwork but easy work with pencils and frowns rather than sinew and bread-and-beer-fueled sweat. Forty hours for fifty weeks for forty years shuttling across turd island, but the kids would save me, they'd inspire me, they'd make me immortal as the stars. Little Jacques and Jan, Sunday dinner of pasta and bottled wine—I'd never drink from a box or a wrinkled bag again.

They were in my mind, the slick green tentacles of the Sending, tearing up memories, feeding doubt and misery, prodding me to join the mass, the hive mind. Animals, humans are just animals, wheedling and baring their teeth for food, cringing from fear of the dark, setting up their clockwork sciences and groaning agricultural faiths, just to keep from looking down. I looked up at the sky, at the *sacré bleu* and was afraid. So massive, so empty, except for one thing. It. The Great Dreamer in The Dark did not fill the sky, It *was* the sky. The moon was gone, those few stars were gone—I couldn't feel the rhythm of the train anymore, or whatever had been poking me in the back from under the tarp; It was all I saw, all I experienced; It was the world and far beyond it. The *atman,* all that is, It is.

I turned away. Memere, living in a faraway anthill, trudging about with the other drones, moving underground in pre-cut paths. But humans aren't ants, there's an order there, a serenity, a determination. People are worse in some ways, full of explosive passions ready to pop like cheap champagne, only a cross word away from fangs or just shitting themselves from the fear of it all. Memere, I couldn't even think of my own mother anymore—not without seeing her as the rutting sow she was, eating and sweating and fucking in the shit of the world, scratching at fleas, finally falling into the rot useless and dead. Animals! And to the Dreamer Of The Deep, dead Cthulhu risen again to bring the world under his sway, we were the fleas on Its back, the shit on Its heel. Jed was wrong, the train wasn't evil. It was that sky that was evil, the vault of heaven stretched over this great country just to mock us all. Hopes, dreams, poetry, the open road, the divine fool Neal, just specks of time and flesh. God damn the sky, God damn the depth of it. I cried deep salty tears, but that wasn't the only salt on my cheeks and tongue. The train was nearing the bay, finally. Sweet, sweet Frisco, Jack is back. The old crew of beat-pigs would surely gather around the pushole metropolis to pay tribute to me, the King Flea, Head Speck Of Flesh In Charge, Bard of the Reeking Shitheap.

I rolled off the tarps before the train even stopped, and I wasn't the only one with that bright idea. The flatbed exploded into a flood of black, red-eyed rats—they tore through the tarpaulin and ran out past the train yard and into the streets, all wiry hair and hot muscle up to my ankles. I ran too. I wasn't sure where I was, what neighborhood. There were hills, crazy-painted houses, palms, empty streets and empty buzzing buses. My lungs were empty husks but I ran, and my hot tongue tasted of day-old beer. I veered right, then left, cutting across streets, legs pumped full of my dead blood. I couldn't see anything but starry lamppost lights for a long time. My feet slapped pavement like Gene Krupa.

Nothing looked familiar until I finally hit the curving

streets of North Beach. I ran past Larry's bookstore, didn't even care that it was still open, and barreled into Vesuvio's. The few patrons, all at the counter, turned to look at me. I'd been running for maybe forty minutes and was soaked in sweat, I probably looked like a junkie who'd spent a week taking pissy showers and jumping out windows.

I slowed down to a casual swagger of a walk and reached into my pocket, just in time to remember that I'd blown most of my money in San Santo.

So I told them. "I'm Jack Kerouac, the famous Beat author, and everyone here has to buy me a round, or I'll die."

Five rounds later, I was feeling a little better. Someone sent for Larry, someone sent for Allen, a few girls wormed their way into the booth and fitted themselves under my arms, all warm and alive. They were good girls too, moral and clean. I wiped my face with a towel and let the spirits settle me down. They told me later that I mumbled for a bit in some crazy holy roller language and then slept heavily. They even swept and closed around me, and left a Guiness for me to wake up to.

Chapter Three

Neal. Neal is... Neal is the smile on Buddha's lips. Neal is not free. Neal is freedom. Running around and writing and loving and drinking and even sleeping. He's a man who can sleep the hell out of a day if chooses to. I'd watch him wile away an hour on a couch and I'd be the one who felt well-rested afterwards. Neal is truly free; it doesn't matter if he's doing time or doing shots, breaking rocks or making time. A childhood spent suckling the poison teat of the state in juvenile halls and reform schools did everything but reform him. The roar of a motorbike, that's Neal. The steam over soup on a cold winter's day, that's Neal. The ball-choked squeal of a maniac undergoing the shock treatment, and the wise old glare afterwards, that's Neal too. And walking away from it all afterwards, that's Neal too; every girl, every drug, every desert wind or smelly city block, the senses lie when they promise either agony or ecstasy, and Neal knows that too and in his starry wisdom he can just walk away from it all.

It had been years since we criss-crossed the country, blessing it like an old woman making the sign three times on Sunday. I was just the midwife for this whole beatnik thing. Neal was both Madonna and Child. If there was anyone who could shake America by the shoulders, and wake it up to the threat it faced, it'd be Neal. He was a bodhisattva himself, I was sure of it then, the one man left who had something to teach me. Neal, sweet Neal who spent two years in prison for marihuana, Neal who had wife now and kids so I heard last night at the bar (or I heard something like that), the last thing you'd expect would be the first thing he'd do. Riding the rumble of the absurdity contraption, the good ol' U S of A, Neal was the one who could do that. All I had to do was find him.

Chapter Four

I was in the john, my head leaning against the cool tile. I had a good night's sleep on a hard wooden table, but the hangover was still outboxing an evening of rest and sweet camaraderie. I had a mind to call Memere, long distance even, or at least sit down and write her a letter when I heard a disembodied voice calling my name. *Jack, Jack* it said, an echoed whisper in the small room at first, then it got louder *Jack!* and happier, a ghost glad to haunt me. I turned, zipped up my pants and looked around quickly for a heatwave apparition or a pink elephant, but saw nothing but grimy tile, myself (that startled me, a flash of my hair in a warped mirror looked like a shoggoth to my bleary eyes), and the firmly shut door.

Jack! The sound was coming from the floor. I looked into the small drain stamped into the floor and saw the glint of glasses. "It's Allen!" Allen said and then he giggled, "Hahahaha, fancy meeting you here." I blushed, then frowned; Allen liked flaunting it sometimes. I reached down, stuck a finger in one of the holes in the drain and lifted the drain cover up. "Just reliving some old glory," Allen said, offering me a toothy woodchuck smile. "Come on in, the water's fine! Hahahaha!" His beard was dry.

"How am I supposed to fit down the drain?" I was still a little woozy. Reality had been giving me the silent treatment for months now, since my breakdown, and the unblinking stare of the Great Old One had done away with the rest of what I thought of as the present actual now. I put my foot against the drain, but Allen smacked my shoe away. "Oh Jack, you're such a card! Hahaha, just go to the closet in the hall and lift the grate. C'mon, we're all down here now. I'll meet you." And he walked out of sight, but I could still hear him under the door, walking out of the space under the bathroom. The hallway had a closet, the closet had a grate, and under the grate was Allen, in tweed jacket and baggy pants.

"Hey Little Tramp," I said, "I'm coming down." He moved out of the way, I leapt down and hit the concrete of the tunnel a little harder than I thought (it wasn't even remotely wet, that's why I didn't hear Allen splashing around beneath me) and hugged Allen. He smiled, hahahahaed one more time, stuck his flashlight under his chin for the scary camper look and then put his fingers to his lips. "Have you been outside," he asked softly, and I told him I hadn't. Had I seen the Beast in the sky—the tentacles, snaky scales, the deep burning eyes? Oh yes, under the full moon and everything, "All the hipsters can see him," he said. "Squares can't, and that's the trouble. That's why we have to move under ground now," Allen told me, and he led me on. There was a downward slope, and the smell of old wet mulch. It was a sewer, but smaller and hotter than I'd always thought sewers would be like. And after we walked a few yards and went down the slope, the walls were old brick and the supports fancy arches.

"Pre-quake sewers," Allen told me. "There's not one system, but dozens, all messed up, running into one another, or into walls of petrified shit. A lot of the tunnels are collapsed, but in North Beach, most of them are okay and connect to all the streets."

"What do you know of Cthulhu?" I asked and he laughed again. "Ahahahaha, I always called it cthew-loo. He's on the money." With that he dug into his pants pocket and pulled out a bill, then shined his flashlight on it. The dead president faded away under the light, replaced with the hideous tentacled head of the Great God, and in an alien font, one barely English, I could see his name carved into the depths of the flat bill. And Cthulhu turned to me, his tentacles dripping off the cameo frame and the borders of the money to reach out to me.

"Where did you get your pronunciation?" Spontaneous enlightenment in a honeybee's buzz, I told him, and then repeated the inhuman name; it was only the second time I'd said it aloud, and realized how weird it was, like my diaphragm had rolled up like a blind and started flapping around. And that was just the syllable with the K in it! Allen tried it and choked on his tongue; I patted his back hard. "Not for the poet's lips, I guess," he said, then he waved the flashlight in my face. I don't think he ever liked my poetry. He shoved the money back into his pocket. That worried me.

Allen led me through a circuitous route under the city. The sewers were a wide shimmy, back and forth and stupid corners built around god-knows-what; and we danced under the whole town it seemed, but at times I wondered if we just weren't walking a dark spiral under North Beach. Even under ground, I could smell the Pacific after a while, when the tunnel began to cool. Allen stopped me in front of a ladder.

"Up up and away," Allen said, "oh hahaha, wait 'til you

see the town proper. There are lots of access holes, lots of *man*holes," he said with an obnoxious wink " 'round here, so if you run into any mugwumps, you can dive rather than take a dive. Oh Jack, hahahaha, it is great to have you back!" He doused the torch and gave me a hug, and slipped a small crowbar into my hand, "For the sewers. The old sewers, the ones you want, have a sort of trapezoid-shaped manhole. Don't bother with the main sewers, nothing but trouble and shit down there."

"Can't you just tell me what's going on?" I asked him and he winked like a trickster and started shuffling backwards down the tunnel. "Would you believe me?" he called out, hollow-voiced and echoing. He was right. I want to see everything for myself, travel every excessive road and collect a smile from every girl and a story from every tramp I see. So I climbed the ladder and gave the sewer covering a shove, then snaked through the portal and into the street by the piers. There was only a drizzle of traffic, which was insane. Where were the stevedores walking off to the bars or walking off their afternoon drunks? The trucks, filled up like a baby with stuffed cheeks, nowhere at all. White-shirted cultists with mandible faces were wispy like ghosts and then it struck me that I could see the bugfaced ones about me, but to one another they were just old pal Harry or Tim the deadbeat who never chipped in for the office Christmas party. Life is drenched with spirit. It rains spirit, we couldn't live without it. But there wasn't a cloud in the sky (just those terrible flailing tentacles and burning eyes covering the dome of the world, so clear, so incredible, *why couldn't they see?*) and this block anyway was full of walking statues, mockery of men.

I spent the better part of the afternoon picking through a few neighborhoods. It was like in San Santos, the bums and tramps and beatnik kids seemed to have souls, some of them were even aware that the mugwumps had taken over so much of the rest of the town. And families, some of the families were all right. Fat Italian mothers and their screaming kids had souls, there was life in flabby biceps, housedresses and great breasts dipping over open windowsills, and in the kiddly shrieks of joy and pain. Some of the Negroes had souls too, old ones embedded in well-worn faces, or in the swirl of strutting shoulders, but I was surprised how many were in the cult too. I saw a storefront church crammed with black cultists, their skin slick with scum and scales, mumbling instead of whooping it up, blood on their hands from palm cuts, puddling on the floor. They didn't notice me. To them, I was the one who was out of step, the fly in the rot too small to even buzz and annoy.

I even pushed open the door and they didn't turn—they would have had it been two weeks ago and a big white man just showed up for a little religion. I walked up and down the small aisle and they ignored me, too busy muttering into the thick books they help open before them. I tried reading over the shoulder of an old woman, the kind of old soul who has a straw hat for every day of the week, but when I looked down at the page, I didn't see words, or even paper. Just a swirling vortex, geometric designs with angles so irregular and rays so strange that I saw the flatness of the page give way into some swirling alien depths. I heard a distant scream, plaintive like a baby just learning fear. Then I realized it was me. So did the preacher.

"Brothers and sisters," he said, his voice a tinny echo in the little store. "We must welcome a lost sheep to the fold." And as one the congregation turned towards me and smiled, eyes warm and soulful again. Welcoming rather than starving. For a moment, I was tempted. I could tell they didn't know me, these fine folks didn't keep up with fine literature or the papers and I'd bet most of them didn't even have a television set. Here even an old Beat Frenchie Buddhist Catholic writer drunk with girl problems could blend in, take his place, be forged anew in the flame of distant Star-Gods and be made moral and clean again. The air was still for a long moment, so still even the flies in the room hovered silently, staring at me with bulbous red eyes.

The preacher raised his codex high (pages flopped and shifted unbound to the leathery folder they were in) and said again, "There comes a time when every man finds himself at a dusty crossroads. On his journey down this lonely road, he is given a choice. A choice to wallow in the filth of the world, to traffic in mud and excrement, or he can take the golden road!"

"The golden road!" the congregation said as one. My limbs were heavy like iron.

"The golden road! The left fork on the road of the billion worlds. Our human nature is sinful but we can transcend it. We can bind ourselves to a higher power, escape our flesh and blood by making ourselves one with something greater, a destiny among the stars!"

"The stars!"

Moving and me were having a bit of trouble getting it together. Fingers and toes were numb and tingling, I couldn't flex my pectorals or even breathe too deeply the fecund air. My diaphragm was pulled tighter than Navy bedding, but at least I wasn't screaming anymore. Light poured in from the storefront's windows, the horrible white light of the dead god now awoke.

"Great Jehovah, God of the Hebrews, even he is from a world beyond worlds. Yahweh, Adonai, most highest and beloved, God and the son of God, our Maker and Unmaker, He is an alien!"

Little steps. My eyes. One eye anyway, the left. I could move that. Blink, I could blink, and the sound of lid meeting lid and then rolling away like old lovers exhausted after a winter's night love saved my life. Blink blink, I blinked. The old woman looked into my eyes, her pupils dilated, but I blinked her away. The call and response, "Gods dead and older than time!" "Older than time!" I blinked that away too, reveling in the song of tiny watery squeaking from my eyelids. My jaw, I could loosen it. I could turn my head, turn it away from this peering congregation of men and women, all short and scaly and sweating, all leaning towards me eagerly, waiting for my soul to surrender the self to the mass. I could turn my head to the windows at the back of the church and I did.

Neal drove by, in an old convertible, top down, some guy in the passenger seat, and a bunch of shovels and rakes rattling away on the thin back seat. I ran out the door, ignored the dozen howling screams behind me and cut to the corner. Neal had the traffic lights with him though and took off through the intersection. I made it to the corner just in time for a bus to pull up and block my view. I looked up through the windows and saw the lunchtime crowd peering back at me, eyes starving, and teeth clenched. All walking dead, sallow and gray as Auschwitz. Some of them were already beetle-faced, but most just had telltale fleshy points on their jowls or cheekbones, or strange wispy phalanges hanging from their chins. Given to the depths, but not yet fully gotten. I cut in front of the idling bus, ran across the street and screamed for Neal, but he was down a steep hill already. The accordion roof over the car's round rear bounced and jiggled, the shovels rattled, then the car turned a tight left and was gone. I looked up to the sky to weep to heaven, but then saw the watery translucence of dead Cthulhu's haunted face and turned my head to the ground, tired and whipped.

I prowled around town for a while afterwards, looking for one of the entrances to the old sewer systems. It took a long time; I had to avoid any block with an office building or a post office—the mugwumps (that's what Allen called them, from Bill's book, I remembered now—damn, I should have read it) were in force there. Not that they cared. Not that they were looking for me like I was a secret agent with a bum full of microfilm in the middle of Nazi Germany, and they were all golden Aryans in armbands and jackboots, ready to stop at nothing just to grab me, chain me to a wall, and extinguish their thin and foreign cigarettes on my chest until I told them what they wanted. I wasn't a threat. Neal might have been though—is that why he was cutting out of town? Off to bury a body in the desert, or dig a tunnel to a sweet freedom underground and away from the blasphemous sky. Or just on the road, carrying garden tools for no good reason to anyone but Neal, looking to get back to Denver or New York. I nearly cried at the thought of missing him, and bit my lip hard, 'til my mouth filled with tired blood. A police cruiser rolled on by, its driver no longer even close to human—it was a great mantis in blue, hunched over the wheel as uncomfortably as a lamppost might be. He… it didn't turn to me. With its black helmet eyes, it didn't need to. I shoved my hands into my pockets and hunched my shoulders, as conspicuous as a little kid swiping his first comic book, and walked in a random direction, eyes lowered. When I found an old sewer grating, I slipped the little crowbar Allen gave me from my pocket, forced open the portal, and slid down into the warm dark.

A bit of setting sun poured in through sewer grates here and there, and walls of lichen that glowed an eerie green were nearly painted down some tunnels, but mostly I had little more than the cherry of cigarette or a flaming bit of newspaper to guide my way, and there wasn't much of a way I needed guiding to. These old 19th century tunnels made my choices for me; one wall was collapsed, another tunnel was so full of stink that I'd need a hillbilly wedding full of wine just to take the first step into it. Only a couple of others were in better shape and well traveled: butcher paper, fresh ciggy butts, pulp and stag rags, and lots of empty bottles. It was easy enough to pick my way back over to underbelly of North Beach. I heard some bizarre and whirling vocalizations echoing through the tunnel, a girly, queeny ululation. I pulled the small crowbar from my pants again and held it like a knife, and extinguished my cigarette against the sole of my boot.

I crouched and pushed myself up against the curved wall of the tunnel and walked, heel first and quiet, like a serial reel Indian, ready to push the tip of the iron right into the throat of whatever shambling horror or mad flailing beast was whimpering and gulping air ahead of me. I was steel run through with veins of hot courage. I didn't need to see a thing, I could smell the horror ahead of me, hear skin rasping against jellied muscle and tar-thick blood. Even the tiny hairs on my arm were standing up and aquiver, like whiskers, antennae. With every step the grip on my crowbar got tighter, I'd loosen my grip and fall off the world. I breathed through my teeth, huffing, my tongue drying. I was The Shadow, the pulp hero I'd read as a kid. He'd lurk in the dark, with ancient Eastern powers granting him the ability to cloud men's minds, and then he'd spring forth, blasting away with his guns, righting wrongs, getting the girl, and with a mighty, echoing laugh, rejoice, victorious!

Then I remembered that I'd never actually killed anybody before. For all the drinking and train-hopping and mix-ups in school and in the Navy, I'd never really done much more than get into a half-fun shoving match with a drunk. Even when I was a security guard, I never bothered to load my gun. It was a grace. I didn't swallow the pain; I never nursed the old childhood rages at being messed with for speaking *joual* with Memere (the kids would surround me, quack like ducks, then run their fingers over their lips—that's what they heard they said). Broken hearts, I mended them with the tiny hands of the girl next door, or one the next county over. I drank with Negroes one day, and nodded through boisterous laughing jokes with Klansmen the next. I embraced all of them, the women, the old men, little kids playing secret games, America was mine. Resistance makes the spirits real, I remembered the teaching now. Embrace the madness with no attachment, something that is both the hardest and easiest thing in the world. I did it with a sigh and then slumped down to meditate in a little puddle. The yelps and oohoohoohing carried on deep in the dancing black spiral of the tunnel system while I sought the no-self.

Massachusetts. Winter. So cold, like the weather was frozen in my little bird bones and just radiated outward from my marrow, to permeate my skin, freeze my clothes stiff, and to steam my breath. I don't remember the snow crunching under my boots, because it never did. I was a light boy, a slim little lad, and snow only crunches in books. The true memory, the real *ti jean* never heard any such thing. He heard, I heard, my lungs in me, breathing hard, expanding and deflating like leather billows. The quacking boys are gone now, into the trees. Every tree hides someone, I decided, right then and there. Some were evil and hiding in wait, or from justice itself. Other trees, the peculiar ones with split trunks or weird leaves, or with sheathes of ivy wrapping, those are where the good people hid. Some from evil, some laying in wait, ready to spring forth with candy or advice or fists of iron, ready to face down the bad boys on behalf of young cats with runny noses like me.

I looked around the field—I'd wandered over the hill and was just out of sight of my house. Memere would be worried. I turned back to the small grove of trees, some good and some evil. I ran towards them, toes suddenly awake and stinging in my wet boots, ready to take cover behind a tree, to decide once and for all who I'd be. Behind a fir, my soul went to the devil, behind a maple, to the angels. I ran so fast, faster than I ever had, ready to take a cosmic side, so excited to be running that I just ran through the grove and forgot to hide behind a tree entirely. I plopped down to my knees, half from the exertion of running so hard in my winter coat and scarf, half from the joy of getting wet and kneeling if I darn well wanted to. I stayed there for a while, watching the white snow turn gray but for the tiniest icy star twinkles as the sun went down. For a long time, until I was darn good and ready, I stayed out in the field, and just as twilight painted the sky, I got up and went home.

Memere wasn't angry when I got home so late, with my pants soaked and then chilled over (I even walked into the living room stiff legged, to show off). Gerard, my brother, had just died. She told me the fever took him and we said nothing. I didn't cry, because I was afraid the tears would freeze on my cheeks. I was seven.

And that memory, that milestone of the self, I lived it again sitting on a puddle in the middle of a haunted sewer, lived every forgotten tear and chilly leaf, then typed it up on the Underwood in my mind, cranked the paper out of the carriage, crumpled it up into a little ball, and then threw it away. A fiction, memory coated with details from books and the demands of drama. That's me, *Jack Duloz*, Jack The Louse. Away.

And without self I stood up, my butt soaked with black sewer water, and walked again towards the huffing and yelping and mad gangster giggling ("heh heh heh heh heh." Edward G. Robinson discovers bennies) with open hands and an open heart.

The purple rose of dusk dimmed the light from the sewer gratings over my head as I turned the final corner and saw Allen. In the splash light of a fallen flashlight, he was buggering some young man, the cat bent over and his curls shaking with each of Allen's thrusts. They were both making the noises, girly and squeaking like old shoes. I'd never quite gotten the etiquette on interrupting homosexual sodomy before, so I just walked up to the pair, looked Allen in his (squinting, ecstatic) eyes and asked just what the hell was going on.

"The" he said, then huffed. "Whole." Another huff. "City." Two thrusts, the boy with the curls grunted, "is…."

"Okay! Stop and just tell me! Send the boy away!" I turned my back on the pair. I heard some shuffling, bumping and zipping up, then footfalls scrambling away up a ringing ladder. I turned back to see Allen there, licking his fingers and dabbing his thick eyebrows, "Really Jack, I'm sorry. You know, I have a problem. A compulsion, it's like a disease, a sickness in me. I can feel it squirming around my spine."

"Not you. Them," I told him, glancing up towards the ceiling, towards The City. I would as soon forget the whole nasty business.

Allen shrugged. "You saw it didn't you? The faces, empty or insectoid. They can't see it. A couple of… friends, have even been institutionalized for insisting that they see the mugwumps. The more straightlaced a person is, the greater the transformation, the deeper they bow to the Dark Dreamer," he said, and bowed low himself, his hands fluttering.

I opened my mouth to say something, to just tell Allen to shut the hell up already and tell me where Neal was going, but he interjected, "It is actually pretty amazing, who hasn't fallen to the Cult of Utter Normalcy, really. The local state assemblyman is a good guy. Must be the time he puts in brainstorming with his constituents down at the…."

"Stop," I said, almost angry, almost full of attachment and desire, but then I smiled. "I understand. So, you're going to hold down the fort here?"

"Spread the madness! Larry's out of town, so is Neal. After he got out of the joint, he… changed. I mean, the man's still fine, still crazy. He just got old." Allen slumped down onto his haunches, "We all got old man. All except you. He's off to Nevada to go open a gas station." Allen nearly spit, "Damn, he wants to support his kids. The *rugrats* he calls 'em! Rugrats, Jack!" I let Neal's rugrats wash over me, then took a step and walked past Allen.

"Nevada. Sodom in the American desert. Gas and hot air. What's the lure, the filthy lucre? I mean, Neal, damn, he can't have gone straight," Allen said behind me. "Jack?" I turned and looked at him, hunched over like a bridge troll, his marionette string shadows playing on the curved wall behind him. His flashlight was burning orange and weak now, like the dimming light of the world. I knew he wasn't going to be moving tonight. Maybe he had a pocketful of pills to keep him up and frantic in the dark, maybe he'd sleep in his own piss or jerk it all night 'til he was bleeding, just to keep from joining the mass of maggots topside on the rotten flesh of town.

"You need any money?" he asked. The tainted money. The cursed money that the Lord's own rats had thankfully chewed to pieces before I stepped on the road again. Money chained Neal to the road, to a pipe dream leading to a roadside filling station in Nevada when he was needed here to fend off the inky darkness.

"No, I own the entire world already," I told him, and I reached into my pocket and tossed him the little crowbar he'd lent me before. I took to the nearby ladder, pushed the manhole cover open with my head and shoulder, then slipped out on the dark and slick streets again. Like the back of a beached whale, nice and slick and curving towards the depths. Ah, it was just another hill in a damn town full of them, but without a lick of traffic. A century of Mother Earth flexing her black and fiery muscles to throw this town off her back hadn't been enough of a hint, so she called in Bigger Brother for reinforcements, and The City just wasn't big enough for the three of us. I looked up again, looked up at the moon, a flaming silver half-lidded eye. He was a big one, the kind of fat schoolyard bully who likes pulling legs off spiders just because little round nubs are more interesting looking than graceful stilt-legs. I stood there for a long time, my neck craned upwards in a staring contest. Tentacles thick as buildings shifted in and out of the fog, pouring from

Cthulhu's chin and stretching out from the sea, brushing the tops of buildings and then reaching out all across this gray land. Go East young man, catch me if you can. But oh I can. My heart was a metronome; I'd sweated out the Benzedrine in Big Sur and calmed my nerves with the tart juice of the juniper berry in sweet, decayed Frisco. The last good bite of rotten fruit. I'd left the ghost of old Gerard in the underworld, along with sick Allen and his last pair of stained slacks. I put out a thumb and by the force of Buddha's palm, a truck stopped for me. Without a word I stepped up and slid into the cab, slammed the door behind me and we drove off, into the depths of America.

Chapter Five

The best thing about riding with a trucker like Ed was his ready supply of solid laughs and a glove box full of bennies. He was taking them by the handful and not bothering with the Coke he held between his knees. "Both hands on the road, eat the yelleh line all up," he said over and again. Ed wouldn't take the new interstates being slapped up; he said that there were too darn many moon rockets being hustled left and right on wideload trailers. "They say they're fer the Reds, heck, they say the rockets don't even exist, but if you see 'un, it's fer to blow up the Reds, but I know betteh. Rockets to the moon. Sekrit bases on the fahr side of it. I see 'em firin' in the desehrt" he said, not once or twice, but every time he took a handful of bennies and chased them with nothing more than the swirling cheekload of saliva.

Me, I drank my share of Cokes and swallowed enough diet pills that I forgot all about California. I don't remember much except for sweaty dreams of missiles firing in the night until we hit Highway 99. The windshield and cab both (Ed liked to drive with the windows open, though he cursed the wind and splattered bugs) looked like Araby from the dust and sand. Ed handed me a hot apple and I bit into it with relish. My hair hurt from being blown so hard.

"Hey," he yelled. "Going all the way to Montana!"

"Nah!" I told him for the third time or so. "Just to a filling station round here."

"That one good?" he said and nodded to an oasis right off the side of the road, six pumps and a restaurant the looked to be named EAT. But the pump handles and hoses had been removed and strorefront windows had been shattered and stood agape like the mouth of a toothless old codger. Like Ed's own mouth.

"I'm looking for one that hasn't been built yet," I said nice and loud, and we both laughed. "How 'bout that one!" Ed cried and pointed to a scraggly bush on the opposite side of the highway. "Or that one!" and his finger whirled. "I'll stop right now!" Both canned-ham hands were back on the huge steering wheel now, and Ed hopped in his seat, jumping on the brake; the truck stuttered with his stupid enthusiasm, "Here," and I jerked in my seat, "or here!" and another jerk, "Or how about here!" and the jerk next to me jerked suddenly too and smacked his paunch into the rim of his steering wheel. Then he leaned back and drove on like he wasn't a jittering freak at all, but just some salt of the earth fellow bringing ottomans to Montana and coffee tables to California, all part of some crazy living room algebra.

"How long you been driving this rig, Ed?" I asked. I smelled something acrid and ashy like a campfire of garbage, the clutch a bit burnt maybe.

"Three weeks. Three weeks Friday." I laughed so loud and he joined me. I couldn't take my eyes off of him. Then he stopped and explained that only a month ago he'd been selling siding, aluminum siding. He'd worked his way up from the crew that'd actually wrap homes in the stuff; he had a good eye and a steady hand, and even better, a wide jack-o-lantern smile and a nervous tick. The tick, Ed demonstrated, was a spasm in the neck, it made him tilt his head and wink and smile wide as the prairie for a second of thick white teeth. Whenever he said something like "Howdy" or "Friday" Ed would have this friendly little spasm, the kind of freak folksy smile that made me want to hand him the shirt off my back, and my pants too.

"So I was really good at sellin' sidin'," Ed explained, his face twitching in robot warmth at the word "really" and oh yes I knew he was really good at selling siding. "But the bosses wanted me to sell more and more, every day," (twitch twitch twice in a row there). "They gaymee a script. It said 'really' and 'very' and 'pardon me' and 'today' and all sorts of other words that set off mah tick.

"But it done gone set off too much and mah face froze," and he turned to me with his wild smile and wink, a face that forgot to fade back to human proportions. The skin across his face was stretched across the bones and bunched up by his right eye. His smile was wide, too wide, like some tough in a bar had taken a knife to Ed's cheek and left a big flapping scar from lip to ear. He held the look for a long time (good thing the road was mostly empty, I could feel the truck drifting across lanes) and then turned away. "Scared the shit outta alla us. It was stuck lahk that for a month or more. But the boss took money outta his own pocketbook and sent me to the doctehr, and he fixed me up. Long needles and ointments and it worked."

"And then they fired you, Ed? Why would they spend all that money on you just to let you go?" I asked him.

"Nah. When I got back to the office, boss didn't want it tah happen again. So he kept me in tah office and I sold sidin' over the phone. But folks just plum stopped buyin'. The boys in tah bullpen were real sorry to see me go though. They said they lahked mah face." And he smiled again, this time for real, a relaxed smile fueled by the joy of the road. He took a hand off the wheel and idly passed his palm and twitching fingers over the dash, looking to corral some wayward pills.

As the day drifted into afternoon I began to worry a bit as so many of the Highway 99 roadside diners and truck stops seemed to be closed. We'd barely crossed the state line by my reckoning, but already some of the little roadside establishments were boarded up; others seemed open at first but as Ed slowed we saw that their windows were darkened, pumps locked, parking lots home only to weeds growing into brush. I didn't want to dip into a town yet, not if even Frisco was set to fall to the demon in the sky.

I remembered too many old towns from my trips with Neal back in the fifties, back when the little burgs of ol' 99 were still half-mad with freedom. One ville I'd never even wrote about broiled away under the Nevada sun, little more than a scattering of buildings around a chain link fence factory. They didn't do anything themselves down in little Compassion, Nev. All the food was trucked in, all the trucks were stuffed with government cash and miles of fencing on the way out, but when sun set and weeks ended, the whole town went a little wild. Old men drove their creaky Models A Fords in crazy eights around the town square. Girls and guys both thumped on iron drums and whooped it up on their porches. On the edge of town, Neal and I saw lizards and brown mice scattering like they'd been called by a Pied Piper playing "Anywhere But Here." Neal kicked at them as we walked past the one lamppost in town and into the weekend bacchanal. Party was religion, between Friday at five and Monday at nine. I even got a day job at one of the bars, lifting drunken managers and linemen up firemen style, walking them across town and dumping the bodies out by the factory gates for a splash of cold water from the foreman's bucket. The mayor paid me off personally, with his wife's pie, plus a handful of old silver dollars and a great and loving handshake.

They don't make towns like that anymore.

Our ribbon of highway was a long stretch of nothing, except for a little wrinkle. A tent, a folding table and an old convertible, and a hill of dirt in the shade. I nudged Ed and asked him to please pull over, and even before he brought the truck to a complete stop, I was out the open passenger-side door, shouting, "Neal! Neal! It's me Jack! Hey Neal! C'mon out!"

And out of the dirt pile he walked, legs and arms loose and swinging. I hopped out of the cab and tumbled to my knees. Neal was already on me, dusting off my pants and shoulders, "Jack! Jack, old chum, old bean, old buddy! It's been…." He stopped and looked away from me, shifty-eyed. Then he turned back, flashing me a grifter's smile. "It's been a long while! How's the book going? Did you get my letters? I still have a bunch of yours." And he ran behind me and both hands on my shoulders started hustling me towards the little tent. "You need to meet my partner too." I turned to Ed. He was out of the cab and urinating on his front tires, for luck or at least for lack of another place to politely let it fly.

So I ducked under the flapping tent roof (the walls were rolled up to better fling dirt away) and noticed a shallow little hole, some maps on a card table and a man snoozing alongside the freshly dug ditch. He had wavy hair, the kind that looks windblown before the wind even starts up, and cheap glasses. One arm was tossed casually outside the shade of the tent and had tanned into a bright gold. Neal woke him up by kicking a bit of dirt on him. "Hey Nelly, Jack is here." Nelly just smiled and nodded though, not bothering even to pop open one eye and give me a gander. I liked that about him, actually.

"So! Let me tell you everything!" Neal started. "God, chronologically. No, too long and ridiculous, in order of importance." He flung out a hand and gestured like a Broadway producer. "This! Is! Your! Last! Chance!" He waved both arms, almost ready to fly. "It's a filling station! You know, I almost called it On The Road filling station, but I thought that might get me into trouble, you know, with your publishers. It'd bring the girls in though—it's amazing how many of them drive past here after they give up their Hollywood dreams." His arm was back around my shoulder, and he turned me back towards the road and waved his hand again in a feverish attempt to transform Ed's long-winded piss against his piss-poor truck into an opium dream of chicks in cars, all smiles and cat-eyed sunglasses, here to ball.

"Neal?" I asked him. "Wouldn't this be the first chance gas station from California's point of view?" And he laughed, that old powerful laugh. The laugh that made him the center of the world once upon a time, and he turned again and shouted over his shoulder, "Hey Nelson, you were right!" If Nelson responded, it wasn't with his voice or body.

"Is that guy okay?"

"Oh yeah—he's been doing most of the digging. I'm more of the idea man. I'm going to make this an A-1 roadside attraction. Hang out here all week, pumping a little gas, maybe helping a motorist in distress or three, then Friday at five, I'll hang up the Closed sign, then roar back into LA. Maybe head on up to the city. Nelson can watch the place on Mondays even, if I'm too hungover or if my babies need me."

"Babies, eh? Are you still with…." I'd forgotten her name. She had had a hang-dog look about her. "Nah," Neal said, before she even came to me. He knew he was far beyond whomever it was I remembered. "I want to settle though. You know, being kept in stir does a number on a body sometimes." He looked up at me again and then his face exploded into yet another smile, this one a warm smile, a grin from his boozy little heart. "You're here!" he said, realizing it for the first time. Then he looked up at the sky, "Boy's really something. Looked like something I scooped up in a net once, when I was down in Baja." I just looked at his chin, flat as an iron. He was shaved utterly clean, the veins in his neck still blue under pasty, pimpled skin. Neal hadn't been out here for long.

Ed in his foghorn voice said, "Hey thyeah, Jack. Ahr yer comin' along or is this tah spot?" I nodded and trotted up to him. We slapped hands, his still sweaty from the slick wheel of his truck, mine cold, tingly. Neal was a little off, somehow. Time and distance and a sky full of madness (and as I shook Ed's hand, I saw Neal was peering up at the sky, not in fear or in wonder, but seemingly in communion. He was rocking on the balls of his feet, like he used to do for Allen's poetry back in New York) had done a little something to him, I wasn't sure what. Once Ed rode off, his truck growling like a fat old dog, I walked back to Neal and looked up too. The tentacles were seemingly right overhead, black and translucent at the same time, and swirling, ever swirling and knitting into one another as they spewed out of a central vortex, a black pit of tiny red stars.

All of this, like some psychedelica splashed over the plain blue and white sky as if from an overhead projector.

"Do you see the constellation?" he asked me, or he asked the sky itself. I just got a look at his nervous, bobbing Adam's apple. "They're alive, you know. The stars. Swirling in infinity. They are the infinity really; they just seem like little sparkles from here, but this planet it just a pebble swimming in between the stars, the matrix." He didn't look at me, but Neal changed his tone, he got all friendly, the Dale Carnegie way. "Jack, you ever draw a connect-the-dots page. You know, of an elephant balancing on one stumpy leg on a platform, and a big beach ball on his tusk. I tell you Jack, connect the dots up there." He smiled, I could see it in the twist of his cheeks, but he was still leaning back, head up, trying to see the whole swirling, dreamy sky at once. "Go on Jack. Keep looking up. Connect the dots. Chaos at the center of the universe. That's all it is you know."

"Neal, c'mon," I said and I stepped forward. Too late already, I thought, my last chance blown. I wanted to tackle him, shove his face back in the dirt, God help me, remind him of his kids if I had to. But Neal heard my footfalls stomping in the sand and he snapped his head back to me, "Don't you see, the country, maybe the world is going mad again! I'll have something to write about." And I laughed. A giggle at first, half-nervous, half-hysterical. "You know," Neal said, "the plane of the earth is becoming non-Euclidean. Jack, we're an hour from Denver now, Jack. Tomorrow we'll be four thousand miles from the same city. Remember Denver? Remember the black mountains that looked like clouds?" He hiked his thumb behind his shoulder, and I looked over at what he was pointed at. Yep, mountains like angry clouds, or the shadow of the Great Dreamer.

"Fuck, Neal, what happened to Colorado? Did it get bigger? Did we get bigger?"

He shrugged, "I dunno. What do you think, Jack?" More grift, more unctuous flimflam, asking me. "Let's go eat on it." And off he walked before I could say yes. I was carried off in his wake back to the tent where he told Nelson, "We're driving up to Mom's. Bring you back a sandwich?"

Nelson stirred, barely. "Rule number one, never eat at a place called Mom's."

Neal turned and smirked, "He says that every day."

"And don't play poker with a man named Doc," Nelson said before drifting back to his little opiate sleep.

And don't drive across country into a maelstrom of shifting sands, deadly cities full of slavemen and snickering queers, along highways lined with drunken babblers and ghost trains, all under horrible bright blue skies with a guy named Neal. We took the car, and on the way to the diner Neal told me of his own brush with the primordial beings, with the demon Kilaya. He didn't get the girl (surprisingly enough, Mary wouldn't stay a virgin around Neal) but instead one of the demon's original forms. A man, Mongloid but muscled, from the torso up. Waist down, Neal said, nothing but knife. Neal was in Mexico, he said ("I went out to get some milk for the kids. It took me six weeks."), and saw the spirit out in the wild brown of some dead field, scratching out a path with the tip of his bodyblade. "It was us, Jack," Neal explained, giggling, "our trips, the way we stitched this country together. It was a message, a sign and a portent, a telegram from God. And then he whispered in my ear." And then Neal whispered in my ear, and it wasn't the sutra that Marie had buzzed before. Neal had received a darker teaching.

He had walked down to the whirling spirit, and not knowing what else to do, bowed down to it. And in the now slowly spinning blades, Neal saw himself. Two reflections, one on each side of the blade. The first good ol' Neal, slick hair, sparking eyes and a voice like a monk's flittering flute. But as Kilaya spun, the sinister side of the dagger showed another image; Neal sallow and deflated, gray skin stretched over deformed, spiked bones. Lips gone, replaced with a huge slash of jagged skin showing off jaws and gums. But in that horrible petrified rictus of a face, power. The phantom Neal's eyes glowed and pulsed with it, his tongue long as snakes and thrashing, ready to kill. And able to kill as well, with a word, with an alien syllable mere humans can't even dream of pronouncing. Neal could do it; he birthed a generation, he could kill a generation—all he had to do was bind himself to the black and squirming chaos in the sky.

"But," Neal said, his face alight, painted orange by the slowly setting sun. "But that wasn't a warning, Jack, it was a promise. Like Kilaya learned compassion and turned to the protection of the dharma, I can. That's why it was sent rather than some other bodhisattva, some old man or baby. The world's changing again, there's power in the skies. We should grab some, use it. Call your big New York agent for me Jack, when we get to a pay phone. Use a whole burlap sack full of quarters if you have to, because we're going to rewrite the world." And with that, we were at Mom's.

The man with the golden arm was right, Mom's was

awful. Brown cherries in the pie, gray vanilla ice cream and flickering lights. Mom's had a jukebox filled with old white jazz 78s, long since warped from the sun and the sealed tin diner atmosphere itself. The speakers sang like weird and distant whales, even the clarinets were deep and made the floor rumble and whine. Neal was drawing a symbol in pepper and salt. "Yin and yang. You can't play the notes without the rests, as you well know." And he placed a pinch of pepper over a tear drop shape of salt. "Sometimes attachment can be best conquered through excess. Remember my letter? The bit about the girl on that bus from, damn, what was it, 15 years ago now? The little perfect virgin on the bus. The way I blew past all the small talk and chitterchat, the way I made sure she was meat for me. A little pink rosebud between her sweaty thighs."

"Wait, I thought you didn't get that girl."

He snorted, "I didn't!" and the symbol of the Tao collapsed in a burst of sandy condiments. I wiped my hands with a napkin. "But I owned the wanting of it, of her. That was enough; I was dejected back then, and of course found another girl a couple of days later," he said as the girl with his bacon sandwich found him and he smiled at her. "But now I am not. The seeking is the thing, not the getting, you know?" I didn't, really. "So," Neal said, "I think I should give myself over to the Dark Dreamer, and then, bound to that power, I can use it to protect reality from the onrushing chaos overhead. Embrace the threat, it vanishes. Resist it, and it remains." He shoved the corner of his sandwich into his mouth lustfully, and spoke through the crunching. "I'll be a dharma protector" is what I thought he said. So I said, "What did you say?" and he swallowed like a snake and said, "I'll be a dharma protector."

He leaned across the formica table like a guy reaching over for a kiss from his teenybopper girlfriend. All that was missing was the shake. "Look at me, Jack. I know you have the gift too. The jazz. I didn't even write my letters in Earth characters, Jack. You never would have been able to read them otherwise. If you didn't have the jazz in you. Look at me, friend. Is there any trace in me? Yeah, I want to settle down, but I'm no mugwump." He wrapped his long fingers around his own throat. "This neck has never felt the noose of a tie."

"I really don't think that qualifies you for bodhisattva status," I told him. Neal's eyes were placid like frozen lakes.

He nodded. "No!" An upraised finger, one of those queer little gestures Neal learned from some cementheaded correctional officer in reform school. One finger could shut up a room of tough little snots. He wagged his index finger at me, and it had a callus. His little Underwood typewriter must have tasted some blood too, when he wrote his letters. "Not yet! But that's the journey, right? A cross-country trip through chaos and cultists, that will be the initiation. We'll see the old, the crippled, the dying, the corrupted twisted man-animals who call themselves Ned and all their bowling league buddies too.

"Jell-O molds. Have you ever seen this stuff?" He grabbed the sides of the table and shook it. My slaughtered cherry pie filling jiggled, and crumbs tumbled and spun in little orbits on the plate. I saw a hair in the mess (great) but Neal was the really disturbing thing. "Gelatin, like bloody cranberry sauce. Everyone's eating the stuff. My kids, Jack! They feed it to my kids in school!" He relaxed and slid his hands across the chrome rim of the table, back towards his own side. “I had to leave, ya know? I just had to recapture the old magic.” Then he looked out the big window. “Nobody needs to buy gas around here anyway.”

“Nobody but us.” There was silence then, except for the popping and buzz of the giant neon MOM’S sign on the other side of the ceiling.

Finally Neal said, more thoughtfully than I ever heard him (and it was sad, when even he felt the need to think before acting rather than just diving on in, a pure spirit), “Maybe it’s not so bad. Is it really any worse than what happened before? People killed themselves for reasons just as foolish. People go to work, stuff themselves full of meat, get down on their knees and wail before something or other, crap out babies from bloody crotches, then feed the worms.” He turned to me with his old smile, “Is it even any different? We’re back, looking for…” and he stopped, tongue out, eyes twisted up thinking, finally like a writer, about what would be the perfect word, “further. And nobody else is anymore.”

“Yeah,” I said, slow. Neal was just a bit too off. He could see things I couldn’t, he knew things I didn’t, and he was trafficking with dark spirits it seemed. The road was mine, this country and this trip were still mine, but those places between the spaces, the breathless vacuum between atoms of air, those all belonged to Neal, that’s what the little Marie-buzz in my ear told me then. “Not so different, not yet. But once we get back on the road, I think there may be problems.”

And with that, it began. The earth rumbled. Glassware and forks sang like a terrified little Greek chorus. The horizon exploded in pillars of flame. Rockets, sleek and curved, like the sketch of a torso, flew up into the purple sky, slow but furious. Dust devils marched and whirled like an army of goblins across the landscape, blind, mad, tumbling into one another, all-consuming and all obscuring, except for the shafts of white hot flame. The far side of the diner was shaking now as the missiles went up in a row, like stair-steps to heaven in the distance. The poor jukebox, already a hothouse of abused jazz, just couldn't take it. The scratchy warbles of the downbeat sped up, sputtered and finally screamed, then stopped, skipping in mid-terror, like a hyena or cinderblocks scraped on their corners against a steel-grated killing floor.

"Ed was right. Like the Tower of Babel, they want the moon. They have no idea what they'll draw down from the heavens, do they?" Neal answered by pushing my napkin into my lap. His he wrapped around his face like an old movie desperado and stood up purposefully, a man about to rob a bank, or at least demand a loan from one. I followed him out of the diner and into the dust storm just as the lights at Mom's went out. The juke croaked out a final goodbye.

Outside we waded through the dust; mostly it just played in whirlpool waves about our shins. Neal stumbled, but I snagged him, and tossed him back up against the wind. Together we made the car and just fell over the doors and into the dusty seats. Neal hadn't put the roof up, but I pulled it up as he tried the choke and after a few minutes of yanking and losing and getting smacked in the face by wind and tarp, I got the old clam shell down. Neal got her going like a purring kitten and wiped down wheel and dash with his napkin. He whipped mine right off my jaw and smacked the dust off the seat with it. Then he stopped and stared straight past the pitted windshield into the shifting sands.

"I think we forgot to pay," he said. The car groaned and tilted to the right, nudged by wind.

"Drive," I said and Neal said where and I said, because America had to be remade and reset, the needle of her hot five jazz record placed on the very first grove again, "Go east young man."

And he did, full speed ahead on a wake of sand, more sideways than forwards, bumping and lurching while the motor grumbled like it was full of marbles, till we found highway again. Then the tires kissed asphalt hard like a well-paid whore and we were off, beyond the wind and sand. In the mirrors, though they were cracked and jagged, we could see them though. Moon rockets in each glass facet, climbing the jewel of the sky. Dozens of them, leaving scorched dead earth behind.

Book Two

Chapter Six

The earth contracted, then expanded again like the belly of a fat and snoring old hobo under a leaky roof. We drove half-blind through Utah, the few miles there were left of it, driving even through the steam that billowed from the red-hot hood of Neal's jalopy. The state was a horrible void of clapboard towns we flew past, cracked alkali flats and squirming horrors only we could see above. The Black Dreamer filled every inch of our vision, tentacles glinting under the moon, mountainous talons sinking deep into the sands off the side of the highway. There wasn't even room for shadow to fall so Neal and I just kept our eyes on what we could see of the yellow line of the highway. When the car was about to fail, Neal cut the wheel hard, sending us into a screaming skid half a mile long. We stopped finally, blocking both lanes of the road. Then Neal got out into the cold night and plopped himself on the hood. It was hot; I could smell the hair on his arms burning, but he snuggled into it and took a single breath. With the exhalation the pain and pressure were all gone, his long nose and ears even relaxed, dropping a bit. Damn we got old somewhere along the line. But Neal was resting like a babe, an opiate smile painted across his face with a single joyous smack of a God's brush against blank canvas. Me, I just stood there shivering in the dark while Neal warmed himself up on the steaming Detroit steel of his car.

It was a huge station wagon that came upon us. It rolled up and stopped about twenty feet from us, idling a low growl, and flashed its brights. I put up a hand and squinted. Neal just smiled on, his eyes closed, his hands in his lap, gentle as flowers. The figures in the car, there were at least four, they didn't move at all. I don't know if they were expecting us to move or just to fall over like cardboard cut-outs, but they were pretty patient. Whiskers of smoke still snaked out of the grill and did a little dance in the aura of the bright lights. Then they spilled out the doors of the wagon and rushed up to me. Still stupid, I waved my arms and said "Hey!" just as the first one, a fellow in black slacks and the most neatly pressed white shirt I'd ever seen, barreled into my stomach. I punched him off, but he hung on to my arm. I kicked, but another guy (same sort of neat shirt) was already there, down low, grabbing at both my feet. One of my shoes flew off. They worked together real well; the first two were just there to take my punches, punches that were too weak from booze and buzz anyhow. It was the big guys from the back seats who really laid into me with big smacking fists. Then firecrackers went off and the biggest one, a monster with pit stains on his shirt, went dead. The others dropped me and howled "Elder, Elder!" and swarmed about the big man, so concerned and worried like babes that they didn't even see that they were bleeding. I stumbled back and from the corner of my eye saw Neal carefully fit a few more bullets into a revolver, aim and fire into the akimbo arms and legs of the suits. Then he slid off the hood and ambled up to the bodies that just weren't quite dead. They groaned a bit. The biggest of them at the bottom of the heap burbled and whispered to the blood in his mouth from beyond the veil.

"Why did they attack me? Were they cultists?"

Neal shrugged. "Either cultists or Mormons. They knew how to work together at least." He laughed. "Maybe they were missionaries! Ha ha, you almost got you some religion, Jack!" I stole a look at Neal. He was haggard and worn but full of static electricity; there were twin spirits in him, like two sides of a dagger, tussling and playing and swapping old stories as they plotted their own little adventure. I was just ballast somehow, I felt, and that made me want to wail.

"You just shot them, in cold blood," I said, trying my best to keep my voice from cracking. I had a big old bruise buried between two ribs from the beating, so it was hard enough to talk anyways.

"I shot 'em in hawt blood!" he said, shouting up at the sky. And he fired again, into the mass of slithering sky. "Speaking of blood, look into the puddle. I'm gonna put our stuff in the wagon. We got to hit Colorado soon as we can." And I looked into the puddle and saw four little souls, masses of cotton candy strands whirled into tiny baby faces, drowning in the black blood. It sizzled against the chilly asphalt.

Without a word Neal made three trips between cars, even loading extra gas from his trunk into the wagon, then got behind the wheel and waited for me. It took me awhile, and not just because I had a few pings and bumps, to get up to the door of the car and slide in next to Neal. I watched the four little souls, so moral and clean, shrivel and bubble away in the muck, 'til they were nothing but pinprick stars. Then I got in, and in a dull, throbbing exhaustion, fell asleep while staring at the yellow line of the highway.

I woke in Denver two days later. We were holed up in Larimer Street and when I finally blinked awake, Neal was gone. Out catting and exploring, probably, rousing the same old hell that fell to rest back when I dragged him out of here years before. Two whores (unpimped, friends of Neal, probably, but we spent two days together in a big old bed) fed me tea and slippery sardines from a dented tin. My head was throbbing and mouth full of ghostly cotton. Every once in a while one of the girls would slide into bed with me, and curl on up. They were so smooth and milk-fed though, Lurlene and Sarah, with curves like warm winter pillows, that my poor bruised body didn't complain.

Lurlene was a quiet type, a dime novel prostitute, windblown and hardbitten in the face, but with a smile for a raggedy man new in town, and Sarah the bubbly one with long curls. She's the one who whispered to me that Denver had gone mad with an otherworldly fever. Obscene blasphemies with naked bloated businessmen and pear-shaped women, their hips and thighs lined with varicose blue lightning, on the steps of the mint, the marble stairs running red with blood. Girls held down and raped in the schools, up against the lockers, not by the boys who are forced to kneel and watch, dicks limp and tucked between their legs, but by the principal, and the black-robed town fathers. The wind tasted of acid and coal dust all the time now because the men of the town—not because they were slaves, but because they all got the idea at once—marched to the outskirts and starting digging. First picks, then roaring dynamite for twenty-four hours a day, digging deep under ground. The night shift rolled through the streets during the day on chicken and hay trucks, shouting for death and the hungry embrace of tentacles.

"And we're landlocked, sugar," she murmured. "These boys have never even seen a tentacle." She had though, back in Chicago, where she was from. The girl was a spontaneous Freudian. She saw I was getting agitated, fired up to take to the streets and do something stupid, some ridiculous glorious act of futility, so she just stroked my hair and kissed my forehead and told me about Greektown, and the little salads she'd get for free from the hairy men with wide smiles and eyebrows thick as shrubs. That's where she'd take her beaus too, back when she lived on the cusp of her old secretarial job and her new gig as very reliable company, and she'd order salads for herself, and for her man. And they'd come, little purple tentacles, all coated with tiny kissing suckers peeking out under lettuce leaves and vinegar-soaked feta cheese, in clear bowls with a leafy design etched onto the glass. And if the boy looked all confused and said, "Well, how do you keep the suckers from sticking to your cheeks?" she'd just smile and say, "You don't. They stick, but just a little," and eat a big forkful of the stuff.

And she did that for months, waiting for some man to just eat the salad without making a fuss, and when she couldn't find one, she left Chicago and came down here for a new life, trying to find a real man or two. "You're a real man, Jack," she told me. I laughed (ah, and that hurt my ribs, even up against Sarah's soft body) and said that she should have just dated one of the waiters at the restaurant.

Neal came in occasionally, sometimes with hangers-on. Beats with wiry beards, young kids in Levis, and girls, almost always a girl, some of them even wearing blue jeans or all black like bad college poets. They'd mutter and talk and compare notes while I drifted between reality and dreamland, where shoggoths still lurked with Marie's face. I never jolted myself awake before the animated ichor of their limbs—a foul discharge both solid and liquid at the same time—wrapped themselves round me, but Neal was always at my bedside on time to prod me awake or cackle and and attract my blurry gaze. He always smelled like booze now, the cheap gin and rum of the biker and down-and-out miner. "Jack, you simply must see the outside world. It's like a thing alive and growing, changing every day. Bloody and screaming, like a newborn or a gook in a rice patty, I couldn't even tell you which. Tonight though, the grim survivors of this alien regime are gonna have a party. You're the guest of honor, Jack, so I hope you make an attempt to sit up if you can. All the arrangements are in hand though, and everyone is looking so forward to meeting you. You're a light unto the dharma, they say. I've gotten Lord knows how many drinks and invitations for a quiet little roll on a creaky mattress thanks to the book. You're destined to be the biggest thing to hit this town since the Rockies!" Then he'd dash out again, talking to himself instead of to me, about how he needed to go to one end of Capitol Hill and make this girl, then come back round the block to meet with some Veiled King and yipping army of man-bats. How he'd need to find a blood-filled bone horn to summon the goblin legions who would carry him in a sedan made of the ribs of babes to the hidden onyx-paved roads that led to the temple of The Blasted One. What can you say but "Good luck!" and wait for the party to start.

And it was pretty good. Most of the guests were human or almost-human toadfolk who slobbered into their own beers (they brought their own keg too; I passed on an offered mug) or Mongloid giants who peered into the apartment through the glass transom and smiled till I wandered over to open the door for them. They just sheepishly went to the corners of the living room and watched. A mugwump named Doc appeared and played poker with himself, a winning hand clutched in each of ten spindly spider arms. A few of the old drunks who knew Neal back when he was a little kid ("I was a real rugrat!" Neal announced as he shoved an old feller named Howie at me, and Howie smiled and showed off a gap in his teeth big enough for a harmonica) joined in the game, foolishly forgetting the old rule never to play cards with anyone who called himself Doc.

I thought a few of the old crowd were there, including Neal's old girl from the first time I met Neal back when the world was young, but it was just a shoggoth sent here to drive him mad. She shimmered on the edges and smelled like a swamp, her eyes were slick as fish. Neal didn't care though he cut across the room like a happy moth and cornered her with a divinely inspired grift. They left together, his arm on her waist and hers stretching like tar on the end of a stick to wrap around his shoulders once, then twice. I eased down next to some little kids who were sitting around a hi-fi in haphazard half-lotus positions, some propped up against the wall, drumming their heads against the thin plaster. New songs, short and simple, bam bam bam on a guitar and drums. Rock-n-roll ain't nothing but strangled blues made squeaking and pale by alien death-grips, and I told them so. They didn't say much in return, but one of them, a boy with eyes blind from bangs and drooping lids called me "Daddy" and then snorted and choked a tiny laugh. They were too limp to do much more than lift the needle (literally, every one of these characters had skinny white string bean arms, the six of them together couldn't generate enough disgust to take the head off my beer) and put on another episode of tribal thump and wail, so I stayed, sitting and listening for whatever love might be between the scarce notes. There wasn't much, but I could sense the heartbeats around me falling into the 4/4 rhythm of the tune, and even my own, still fluttering from a handful of bennies washed down with brew, stumbling and seizing to join them. When a record would end (little 45s, is there even room for art on those few grooves) the pasty little nuggets wouldn't even talk about the song, or nod or say how good it was. They just put on another, like librarians alphabetizing books. So I up and left, caught in the wake of some young thing with legs up to her neck, butter blond hair down to her knees and a walk like a cowboy. She was in boots in jeans so tight she must have been greased when she slid them on that morning. In her pocket was a dog-eared paperback. I caught up with her, slipped the book out and into my big palm and held it in front of her. Pretty girl she was, she smiled small, showing just a few rounded teeth between her full heart lips.

"Any good? It's good to see a girl read around here, I'll tell you that. Sometimes I wonder if girls want anything to do but marry, you know?" She nodded, her eyes glancing away from me like a little bird. "Yeah, I like it. Everyone's reading it these days. It's very…" she sucked in mile-high mountain air, then conjured up her adjective, "inspirational. It's what led me here to Denver." Excited now, her girlish hand squeezed my arm. "I love this city. Can you believe this party, just like the one in the book!" I turned my wrist to look at the cover (probably should have done that first) and it was my book. I couldn't help but smile. "Heh, I think the party is a bit different these days, what with the strange characters here now." She snuggled up to me and turned to one of the pages with a folded-over corner. "No, look. See?" And there it was, in my book, the mugwump poker, the dumb mods huddling in a corner, Neal, his pants down to his ankles, taking his piss out into the heaven-upturned bowl-mouth of a shriveled woman no longer than a foot tall.

"Read me some," I told her and put the book to her chest, "out on the porch." I hustled her out of the pad like a nun on a truant schoolboy. There were sizzling rocket trails netting the skies, some headed up, others down and around, tracing the oval of earth. Even in Denver, you couldn't see the stars anymore through the streaks of smoke and flame. Purgatory had snuck up somewhere between heaven and earth. Even the moon was reduced to a scattering of haze, but there was an old bulb on the porch roof that you just had to turn (and just had to go "Ah!" and pull your burnt fingers away after it sparked to life, and I did both) to get light so she could read to me her favorite passages. And she read them. The show-down with the cult deep under ground, a pulp fiction shootout, ol' Moriarty crying over his writer's block till his eyes ran black with blood (he'd made his soul a gift to the wrong muse, it said). I just didn't remember writing any of this yet, and didn't remember reading it for big wads of cash before auditoriums full of serious-minded young men and women, the sorts who ironed their collars just to look neat when the time came for them to wear iron collars. But I let her keep reading, because her voice was honeyed and just so interested, she brought out the secret reasoning behind every clumsy word. She sang the stuff really, and so well we didn't hear the sirens until they circled the block like Indians. In the red-and-white moment of the police lights I looked up and saw the new brute squad. Street thugs in burlap sack and hubcap armor over business pants and smart cop shoes (black but not dusty, they shone in the otherwise smoky haze of night), and a mix of ten-gallon hats and paddy caps. "Uh oh, I don't think they're here for the party," my honey girl said but I couldn't think of another reason for them to show up. She put the book back in her jeans before I could filch it from her and walked backwards on her awkward heels till she was inside. I just smiled and gripped the porch's railings and called out howdy while they carefully took up positions around the house, behind convenient cars and across the street.

"Anything I can help you with, officers!" In my mind's eye, I saw that they were all human, not a trace of the mugwump in them. Neal was at my side, holding up a piece of typing paper, "Check this," he said, excited as if he'd finally gotten around to writing something. He folded it in half, lengthwise. The cops, or maybe just dress-up civilians making do, as they didn't stand like cops, dug into their weird costumes for their revolvers. Some of them had little snub-nosed .38s, others held big monster guns, the kind the old Denverites liked to show off, cradled in big callused hands like sweet babes. Neal folded the paper in half, and then in half again. "I don't really think this is the time for an old magic trick," I said. Someone blew Neal's mind once, back in reform school, with the old saw that you can't fold paper in half nine times. Near every time I'd finally sit him down in front of a typewriter, I'd leave him alone for an hour and come back to a room full of flapping little pieces of paper, all blossoming out from his half-hearted folds.

The Keystone kavemen kops surrounding us were half-hearted too, but it doesn't take a murderer to make a killer, and I was starting to grip the porch a bit too tightly, flecks of paint melted into my palms. I tried calling out to them again, but they ignored me utterly. Neal folded the paper twice more; it was a tiny little block now held between fingers and thumbs. "Watch, Jack, watch me," he said, like a little boy. He folded it again, easily really, though it was a stiff accordion pile in his little fingers now. I wished I'd brought my beer out here, my throat was too dry to say a word. I could only see them shooting Neal first (because I had to be alive to see him fall) and a bullet cutting through that stupid piece of paper, blasting it to dust and flakes to drift dramatically over our blood-Pollack faces. Neal was whoopin' about something and two of the cops had rushed up to the porch and started splashing smelly gasoline along through the rails and onto the floor. I knew, somewhere deep in my reptilian brain, the fight or flight or fuck part that attached me to this damned world, that if I kicked at them or even shouted for help I'd get a bullet in me. Of course, burning to death wasn't shaping up to be a great way to end the evening either, but the possibility just seemed distant, like the long wait for a motion picture railroad train to burst through the screen and plow engine-first into the orchestra seats, its flickering black-and-white smashing into the real colors of the world.

"See!" Neal said, holding a weird wad in his hand. "Ten times folded! It's a new world we're living in. If we dream it, we can be it, all while the Dark Dreamer himself looks to kill the dreams of all humanity!"

"Great," I said. I couldn't look at him without seeing

the blood speckled across his forehead, a huge pulsing cavity, a still-living heart within, where his chest would soon used to be. "We're going to die now, I think." And Neal laughed, an "ahahahahaha" almost like one of Allen's, and ducked low. He slipped his arms between the rails and dug the fingers of both hands into the ground, then looked up and gave me that country smile, slanted on his face. "Watch!" he said and with that tore the country apart. The ground ripped like sails in the wind and the cops and cars and even the smog from a hundred rockets just went. Off into some non-being, a dark non-being, the black reflection of nirvana bliss. Just black, like space without stars. It lays under the earth like a lover under a blanket, naked and waiting. Then the rift was gone and the street just empty again, asphalt, concrete, then the brown grass of the tiny stripe of lawn in front of the porch.

"Lord God, you see that," Neal said, standing up. He made to dust off his hands on his pants, but they were clean as though he'd never dug into the dirt. "That was beautiful. When the Buddha smiles, he's opened mouthed, you know, Jack?" Neal nodded, more to himself than me. He was electric again, the world shifted a bit to make sure he was the axis about which it revolved. "White teeth are just a border surrounding a deeper dark portal, into…."

"Into the belly!" I said, then I blushed when Neal didn't laugh, when he didn't even hear. I shamed myself, a fool who lets his booze chatter away for him. I prayed for the bullet and the shower of blood now. Neal went on though, gracing me with presence and wisdom, the sort of thing I blundered into by simply following in his footsteps. "Something greater than the self, that's what's been missing. The mugwump slaves have been looking for it, but it was the Holy Fool who found it, ya know?" But if he was a holy fool, I was just a damned one, that's what I figured anyway. Then he turned and embraced me, "Jack, Jack oh Jack, that is what I can write!" And with that, I just had to hug him back. "You still have to teach me, you know?" I didn't know that, but why not, I thought. We went back into the party and slowly watched it dissolve. The pain of ending hung over it already, but the guests struggled against death like a note fading before the needle finally hits an absent groove and ends it all. Monsters lurked in the corners, just curious and getting a kick at being around a few folks who had their souls still sealed tight in their gullets. The true human stragglers didn't make much of a spectacle of it, they drank till their bodies made them stop, and drifted into their solipsistic little dreamlands, the mommy and daddy dreams of someone who has never been beyond the veil where Great Old Ones wait and plot and go mad. That cute girl cut out when the cops came, one of the moptops told me, out the back door and back into the warzone of Denver.

In the morning, I woke up on the couch. A seven-foot tall man, his head an anvil and eyes just slits, sat slumped in the corner, his knees as high as I am tall. The other guests had picked their way home. I got to the kitchen and brewed up some coffee and found some cheese and bacon for breakfast, and ate alone on the little tin table the whores had picked out of the garbage. Lurlene was in the backyard, body still as tough as a cigar store Indian's, hanging up the sheets I'd sweated into for days. I'd miss her, even though we never talked. We *knew* one another, and that was enough. Who knows what I really gave her that night, in the language of friction and little kisses? There were no napkins so I just wiped my hands on my pants and went looking for Neal, and to say goodbye to Sarah.

Hadn't even seen her at the party. It wasn't as good as the old days here in Denver; the magic was gone. All the old crowd had left years ago, or had desperate families holed up in little homes now. In the living room, the Mongoloid thing was gone too. I stood there in the empty room for a while, then walked out into streets painted orange and violet by the low-angled sun.

Chapter Seven

I spent the afternoon on a flatbed truck with Neal and a few old tramps who wanted out of town as bad as I did. In a minute or two, I think I would have been happy to stay because the argument on the bed was getting heated.

"It smells like shit!" Neal said, and that was that, a tentpeg pounded into the earth. One of the fellows though, an archetypal tramp, a guy who wandered out of dreamland with a bindel and pants baggy enough for two, just wasn't having any of it. "Smells like money," he pronounced, with a lifetime of road lore and an eye for cattle to back him up.

It was shit, the shit in streams and sumps and coating the asphalt of our poor, half-shattered highway out of Colorado. Ranching territory stinks to high heaven, and it isn't just the dung, but the very air around the cattle. The old tramp joked that if Neal lit one more cigarette just to throw the cherry-red butt out into the wind, the whole half state would go up in a bellowing holocaust. "Hamburger for everyone!" he said and laughed a hollow little laugh. The other tramps murmured not so much agreement as they did a general sentiment that a hamburger would be quite nice right about now.

Tramps and hobos were drawn to the languid shit swirl of Colorado's ranches, but only the hobos would work, bailing hay or twisting nasty barbed wire into mile-long swirls. The tramps took after their bug-eyed fly brothers, filching a cooling pie there, shoveling sloppy handfuls of cool pump water into their cave mouths here. There was cash to be had too, all you had to do was cut the pocket of a hobo on siesta and get to the highway and to a passing truck before the hobo got to you. Not even the greatest of tramps would dare beg or molest one of the ranchers these days though, they'd as soon shoot you as look at you the old man said, and crush your corpse under the hooves of their Arabian horses and feed the meat-sauce mess to their prize milk cows.

"Ain't the milk been tastin' funny lately?" he asked another tramp, one who probably hadn't had a cool glass of milk since the Depression was on. "Now you know why!" Our second tramp, a man with a two-axle spare tire and pants split in the front nodded. "Yep. The ranchers have burrs in their asses these days, The cattle too, they're all ready to stampede. You can see it in their eyes." Neal just snorted though and nodded towards a few fat cows chewing their cud off the highway. "They look pretty placid to me," he said, and flicked a cigarette butt off the bed with his speedy fingers. Then he was back to his journal, scribbling away and muttering about how it did so smell like shit, shitty money even.

I looked at the cows, my eyes focused past them at the fading horizon so that the Third Eye could peer into their little animal souls. Sweet and innocent they were, not even their shit was tainted with the rot of the Dreamer yet. The lighthouse was another story. "What the heck is that?" I asked the wise old tramp and he told me with the clarity of a sage, "A lighthouse." Fatty knew a bit more of the story, as he sang for his supper among the masons who had put it up over the past few weeks. "A gentleman from Providence, a jaundiced fellow it seemed to me, he came out here some weeks ago and ordered it built. He had men working around the clock, under huge and roaring bonfires so they could see in the night and labor unmolested by the swarms of biting insects who usually feed on the cattle in the night fields. Taciturn man, like Yankees tend to be. He didn't have much time for an old tramp," he said, his voice resigned but still lyrically thick. He could spin a tale when he had to, a tramp doesn't get that fat otherwise. "But one time, I did get up the courage to walk up to him. It was a prime opportunity, because it was a Friday and even Mr. Love gave his workers a bit of a break for some cool beers on Fridays, though he never drank himself. But he had a half-smile and tip of his hat for all the boys, so I knew he might have a word or a coin for me. I didn't get a coin when I introduced myself and told him my particular tale of woe, but I did get a word when I asked him why on earth he'd spend a whole wheelbarrow full of gold just to build a lighthouse a thousand miles from the nearest ocean."

The fat old tramp sucked on his gums then, and gave the little tuft of hair on his gut a scratch. "And he had just one word for me. He looked at me, his eyes so round like a frog's, opened his lipless mouth and said 'Wait.' Just like that: 'Wait.' An eviction notice for the West."

Neal laughed at that one. "Oh, that is rich, friend! That is going into the book! Finally, the big one will hit and California will fall into the sea. I read all about that when I was a kid. The whole state will fall to pieces. Fissures of fire tearing apart the streets!" he said, and without another word, he was back in his pages, composing paragraphs on the spot.

My stomach shifted uneasily, and not due to the shit in the air. The road had taken on a little downward slope, and the tramps and I all gave into it and slid like little kids a foot or two down the length of the flatbed. Neal stayed rooted in his full-lotus, notebook in his blossom lap, writing away. He even ignored the inevitable ritual of the bottle. Cheap rye burned my throat but eased the electric jangle of my poor nerves and muscles. My whole body was hungry, every pore was pulsing and crying out for something. A lay, a pill, a bath of gin and slippery little fingers, a damn plate of spaghetti in a West Village dive, something of this world in me. Rye would do it, but if it wasn't for the rye, I'd be ready to eat pages from Neal's journal just to know that my insides were still there. At least, I thought to myself (as opposed to the dharma itself, which I now realized one could also think to, so I also thought to my last memory of Marie, her naked body falling like silks and leaving only a hovering bee behind) I was hungry for something rather than hungry for nothingness.

I was hungry for Neal, for our old conversations, for the big times we had and for all the folks who'd get caught up in our wake. I thought I was going to lose him to the crucible of prison or to the workaday world of dandling rugrats and frowning over report cards. But it wasn't that. Neal was lost to some darker matter. We were the little eddies of life in the frothing wake of the horrible Nothing that had wrapped around the Earth. The pull was an inversion of gravity; I couldn't turn my face from the sky even had I wanted to. I looked over at Neal, the buoy on this dark and writhing sea, his nose buried in his book, his fingers red and wrapped around his ball-point pen. He didn't feel the pull, he had let those tentacles wrap around him and pull him up into the mad and starry space. But he came back, seemingly unscathed, and now he just sat and wrote whispered prophecies and pulp fiction like one of his rugrats scribbling with a wax crayon—I couldn't believe he wouldn't show me even a sentence of his book. As we rolled into the heat of tiny Goodland, Kansas, he silently decided to nap, and used his notebook as a pillow. The tramps smiled at him, not mean or with malice, but like Neal was their very own babe in arms.

The citizens of Goodland weren't so sweet and gentle. When the truck pulled up to the weigh station and waddled out, nobody noticed his thick beetle jaws, or the head of writhing maggot hair that dripped into a squirming trail behind him, like the tramps and I did, but they just didn't like him anyhow. Or they didn't like us, the friendly old joes who had taken advantage of the somnambulant shuffle of the missile corps to get a ride into their quiet little oasis in the hot fields of this very square state. I even got a pair of frowns from the little birds who were working summer jobs behind the lunch counter. A blonde with hair piled high on her head and held there with bobby pins thick as handcranks flicked her wrist to toss a plate with an underfed sliver of pie on it in front of me. It spun and rang against the counter before settling down into the silence of the little establishment. The cook, a big old slab of pork, kicked his way through the swinging kitchen door and held up the far wall, just to stare at Neal and me. Except for a telltale coating of rancid sweat, he was a human, and so were the girls, and so were the grumbling farmers (even the fellow who must have lost four fingers to a thresher still had his soul intact, if gray and withered).

Neal noticed the nasty human stew we sat in and said a bit too loudly, "Whooee, now here is a town of people who go to church on Saturday nights too, isn't that right?" It was too hot for a fight, so we didn't end up in one, but I made sure to eat my pie in double forkfuls (I'd been eating so much pie, just like last time I was on the road, but now the cherries were all strangely bitter).

"You're all going to die you know," Neal said, not to the room. He sat on his stool and talked to an imaginary waitress, the casual flirtation of a madman. "Don't think you'll be allowed to survive, it just isn't up to you. Specks of meat and time." He quickly undid the buttons on his left cuff and rolled up his sleeve, fingers twisting and spinning quick like snakes. "Look, see?" he asked the air (and the air grew hotter and darker as the patrons' grousing tainted the whole scene—it was the mumbles of war). "Look, do you see this? Do you see this FLAKE of skin? Does it get a vote if I throw myself into a wood chipper? No." Calm again, he rolled his sleeve down and took his elbows off the counter. The big cook, preceded by his majestic paunch, was right up against us, his breath a furnace, all rotten beef rounds and huffs of steam. Neal slid off his stool and hugged the old bastard. It was a gentle, liquid hug too, around the fellow's pear belly; cook's meaty arms were still free, he could have crushed Neal's head, or pushed him away or even just returned the hug in his manly little way, but he didn't.

He started to cry. Neal smiled his own mother's smile at the cook and then buried his head in the old man's chest and squeezed. The murmuring and shifty-eyes of the few customers faded into the ogling of comic-strip slackjaws. Slowly, like continents drifting, the cook's arms moved up and out, a shift with all the grace of Martha Graham but without the effort. Like his arms were made for this and nothing else, up and out. There weren't a million lifetimes of cracked flint and strangled pigs and bricklaying and murder behind the design of cook's limbs, there was just his embrace of Neal, bones and sinews all forged for just one hug.

"I'm sorry you're going to die," Neal said, soft like a child. And the old cook nodded his elephant head. "Don't feel bad." He was solemn, wistful, and his accent sounded like a steel-pedal guitar's plaintive wail, the song after last call. "You're going to die too." And with that I cut to the door but it was chained shut. Behind the counter my waitress pulled the key to the thick old padlock from her cleavage and offered up a sad little pout. Sorry to see us go, I guess. Neal and the old cook still embraced as the others collected their hats or dug in their pockets for tipping dimes. Everyone seemed pretty bummed out; they were the folks who didn't get the last piece of cake, or maybe the Little League team lost to their rivals in tiny Goodland *Junction.* These folks weren't murderers or slaves to the red stars of Azathoth (how many threads of fate did the new constellations burn in their nuclear fire?), they were just suncrazy and pulled a short straw or two somewhere along the line. Me too.

"It's okay, Jack," Neal told me. He was still hugging his new friend. "Everyone dies. The soul is immortal. This isn't even real; it's an illusion. The world, it's a mad dream of a blind god. These poor fools do not know what they are in for." For a moment, the truth was enough. The stasis of the roadside diner collapsed into the shimmying of spinning atoms, of the spirit wave *chi* made flesh and stone through nothing other than half-wit conception. We beg for the world of matter, then weep when we get buried under it. Didn't stop my heart from rattling around my rib cage like a crazed rat though, and two strong men had to grab my arms and twist them around my back while the waitress opened the door. She grabbed Neal's gun from the inside pocket of his jacket when he passed, arm in arm with the cook.

They marched us across town (Kansas isn't flat; we dipped and soared, crippled birds being put out of our misery by some tom cat) and tried to explain themselves in low tones. It wasn't them, not them at all. It was the others, the folks who work in town at the bank and the insurance company, the mayor and the police, they were to blame. They were the ones with beetle lips. One day they just surrounded the little brick schoolhouse and would let the kids come home. "They're safe now," they said, mandibles clicking between words, a sound loud as an axe sent into rotten wood. The big farmers on their outskirts of town were no good either; they had their kids safe and sound except for the greenish-black taint on their skins; like those damn kids and their folks who drank too much swamp water. Jimmy Barber went down to the school with his rifle to get his little girl back, but he didn't make it within a hundred yards of the place before the air turned to razor wire and cut him into luncheon meat.

And all the new town fathers and mothers wanted was a pair of drifters of our peculiar description, down at the square, to be sacrificed at dusk. The old cook, speaking conversationally enough to Neal, told him that he had been a butcher boy back before the war ("Which one?" Neal asked. The coot just laughed and said "The war to end all wars." Neal asked if he meant World War II then, and the cook just laughed and said "Nope, prior to that 'un.") and that he'd do well by us. "No pain, no muss. Your wallets won't even get damp. I'll do you boys in a slice and send you to a better place than this. I'm terrible sorry about all this, but I know you'd do the same."

And Neal said, "Oh yes. I'd do anything for my children too, I know it. Lord knows I should have settled down much sooner than now. They'd be better off, and damned if I don't know that I would too." I wondered about little Jan but felt nothing but death in my chest. I didn't see her but for a few minutes last year—moon face and dark hair, that was her. What do you say to some little person like that? "I'm your poppa, well, see ya around!" That's what I said, I guess, and would have left it at that, but my own blood told and my agent cuts checks on account of me cutting out.

I raised my head and looked about. We were heading to the town square. The same old clapboard houses and storefronts that pimple this land, but different. Weird, like Dali, some of the buildings were melted around the edges, huge drops of wood puddling on the corners. The dirt blowing 'cross the road was redder than rubies, and the road, damn. To use a cliché, it really did flow like a river. The men yanking me along didn't even move their feet, but just floated and bobbed as the road took us where we were headed, our final reward I bet.

"Where are the beetlemen?" I asked.

"Too close to sunset. They only come out under the sun." He chuckled. "Maybe they're scared of the dark," and for that, the lump of a man on my right shoved me into the talker. I made a pretty fair elbow, because the talker returned the favor and pushed me into his pal. Like two kids, they started jerking me around as he we flowed down towards the center of Goodland, yukking it up and snorting. Finally, the old cook turned around and barked,

"Hey! Respect for the dead!"

And we were there, the sky just about to purple. Neal went right up to his stake and smiled at the old woman with owl-eye glasses who tied him with old twine. I got smacked up against mine, and the Bobbsey Twins tied me real tight with thicker rope; it burned as they tugged and yanked on it, as they played with each other like I was already dead. When would Neal act? When would he dance out of the ropes and tear a vengeful hole in the sky, one that would just swallow Goodland up and leave the two of us here alone by our stakes? I looked over at him, and he wasn't smiling any more—he had the look of a saint about him, the poker face of a master bluffer who actually has a royal flush, but wants you to think he doesn't.

"Last requests?" It was the waitress. Behind her, a scattering of townsfolk, all human and oh so sad for it. None of them could stand to even give me a decent look; they all either cast their eyes at the ground, or turned to check out the setting sun. It couldn't sink too soon for them.

"Whiskey ought to do it," I told the girl. Neal just smiled like a saint and said, "Peace."

"Sorry," she said, then sighed. "Goodland is a dry town." The creak and whirl of a sharpening stone started up behind me. In my mind's eye I could see the cook pedaling with one foot, and maybe raising one of his steely knives up to the sky to see it glint, perhaps chuckling at the thought that this town was dry. His basset hound eyes told a different story; in basements, at night, 'round stills or poker tables full of beer bottles driven in from the next town over by the sheriff's son, he drank his fill more often than not. He drank just enough, I hoped, to keep him from crying too much after he killed us. He didn't drink so much, I prayed, because I didn't want his hand to shake when he laid the blade against my neck. Car tires squealed in the wind, someone escaping with a school kid bundled up in the back, or just another tourist who'd curse an empty diner and drive right on past our scene and find the highway. "Dry town, that's so funny!" Neal suddenly said, and he laughed with a stutter. "Oh yes, it'll be wet in a minute though, wet with blood!" His eyes were wild, and his tongue flicked across his lips. Behind us, the cook said, "Settle down, son" and the scrape of his wheeled stone died down to nothing. Even the waitress turned away from us now. She didn't see a thing when the shooting started, but fell right over, the top half of her head beating her to the ground by an even half-second. The cook went next. I knew because I felt his blood hit my hands and hair and I heard him thump down like a pig he'd just stuck. Most of the others managed to run off, but a few got picked away, heads blooming with blood, legs managing to run a step or two before getting the news that they were already dead and finally folding like a marionette with cut strings. The streets of Goodland echoed with the reports of gunfire; my old friend of a thug ran the wrong way and into a bullet, one that sunk right into his forehead. He fell cross-eyed, trying to see what just did him in.

Finally, after the crack and thunder of guns stopped ringing in the street, Bill Burroughs walked up to us, his face still hangdog and sallow like I remembered. His hair was swooped over and damp from sweat, the peculiar sweat of the junkie that Burroughs always looked like he had just been dipped in. In his hands, he carried a pair of long pistols. Bill hadn't shaved in a few days and didn't smile when he saw us. He just said, "Fellas?", more a question than anything else.

Neal smiled. "The Old Bull! I knew you'd make it. I

tried to tell these fine upstanding—well, they're downbleeding now—but I tried to tell these citizens that they were going to die. They just didn't believe me. Not even old cookie."

"Burroughs, untie us please," I said. Haven't had much use for Bill lately, but I was ready to hug the old queen. He shrugged and tucked his guns into his waistband like an old movie cowboy (or like someone who wants to be sure that he shoots his pecker off—if one don't get it, the other gun will) and untied us silently, like he was waiting. Neal was just pleased as punch, as happy that Bill came in and blew away seven people who were ready to carve us to pieces as he'd be if he just saw old Bill half on the nod and staggering down the streets of Frisco.

So I asked, "Damn, how did you know? How did you know to come out all the way to Goodland, armed for bear, just in time to save us from some sort of sacrifice." My binds fell and Bill threw the ropes to the ground. "Neal wrote me a letter a few weeks ago, telling me to meet him here. He said there was something important for me to shoot. Doesn't seem like it, really," he said, his voice just like a frog who can't swing. He took it slow, wandering more than walking over to Neal, and untied him too. I looked around for the old lady; she wasn't among the bodies. I guess she got away somehow—did Bill even aim at her, or was she lucky? Real lucky, yeah, like all God-fearing folk of Goodland, who just want to live their little lives under the spiked and hooved boots of their horrible alien overlords. "How'd you like the old William Tell routine?" he asked, but if he meant that question in dark humor his voice didn't betray it. Bill really wanted to know. I didn't want to tell him, I wanted to think of something else—anything other than those poor fools falling to the power of the gun.

The kids, I thought, and that surprised me, because I thought it the same time Neal said it: "The kids!" And in the space of one horrible breath, another gong sounded in the distance and I saw the truth. There were no hostages, just a school full of little bodies, all wrinkled and thin from the rot. They'd just been locked away and starved, wailing and whining for mama. Then they got nasty with each other, the boys holding down the girls and eating their hair and biting their skin, just to have something to eat. The beetlemen didn't have to torture the little tykes, those sweet cherubs with their cheeks rosy and slick with tears. They already knew the tango of life and death. They ate their own crap, and the paper, and chalk, and drank pee and then just upped and died, bodies so little and so desperate to grow that they burned themselves out.

"We have to save them!" Neal said, frantic again with the wave of a new idea. "They took my pistol, Bill, give me one of yours." He reached for Bill's pants, but Bill sidestepped and held up his hands, "Neal, really. I passed by the school. Remember? It was in your letter too. You already know…."

I knew too, thanks to the buzz of Marie-bee, the demon who told me everything she felt I needed to know just days ago in Big Sur. The Goodland cult got no pleasure from those kids; they didn't torture the third-graders for secrets, they didn't drink sweet young blood like nectar; the mayor and the fire chief, the banker and the librarian, they just surrendered their souls to the Dark Dream and forgot. They forgot that babes need to eat, that they need hugs and baseball and to be told to wash behind their ears or else they won't do it. Some demon impulse told them to collect the kids and trap them behind a spell that could turn the air to a wall of whips. And then, nothing. The cult knew its place was in the stars; they spent their days dancing under the writhing invisible tentacles that filled the sky in their offices—every paper pushed a celebration. And their nights, oh the nights. Evenings the cult spent in their homes, puppets acting out a shadow life, just to make sure everything looked normal. Act natural, the bleary-eyed god from the sea told them, and the good folks of Goodland don't step outdoors at night. So they stayed in, and nobody even thought to bring the children food, and the kids burned with hunger and then with rage, then they howled and died.

Neal knew too, once, in a burst of ecstatic prophecy, but now, back in the mundane world, he had to go see for himself. Bill and I just stood around, not saying much, while Neal yipped and ran off, collapsing in a heap, and then running off around the corner to where he thought the school was. A minute later, just as Bill was opening his mouth to say something or other, Neal ran by again like Harpo Marx, heading in the opposite direction. Bill shut up at that. I rubbed my wrists raw and waited—Neal would be fine. His special sight would show him the whirling blades that surrounded the school and he could pick his way through them, ducking and hopping and rolling, as easy as you please.

The looks on the corpses' faces were just unbearable. It wasn't even the fear that lasted like rubber cooling in a man-shaped mold with eyes and a nose, it was the disappointment. The cultists had told them, after all, they it would all be okay. No more empty spaces at the dinner table, no more empty Sunday School (heck, their prayers would be answered in a way they could point to for years later—"Yep, and then Clem was returned to us, just in time for chores, hale and happy as you please") and all they'd have to do is find two strangers and butcher them. That's what they were disappointed in, these bodies, the hard fact that life wasn't fair. One woman, Bill had shot her in the neck, so I could still see that her mouth was a line of desperate consternation, she had a novel written in her expression. *Come on, Cookie,* I could see her screaming in her mind, even as the bullets rained down and the other members of the Ladies' Auxilliary fell on either side of her. *Kill them! Kill them with your blessed butcher's knife and the bullets will stop. Kill them and Alice will be home by the time I run back there, and we can all have supper like a family again. Life isn't fair,* she finally realized as a bullet ate its way through her in a split-second. Life wasn't fair, and not because Neal and poor old me were trussed up and about to be skinned alive either. Life wasn't fair because even the soul-raped slaves of the Dreamer In The Darkness couldn't be counted on to keep their promises, and to let their babies go free, safe and sound.

Soon Neal came back eventually, when the moon was bright and high and his head low, hands in his pockets. He walked up without saying the word, and I swear, that was the first time I'd ever seen Neal sober and speechless at the same time. Even his head, when he lifted it, even his chin that drooped just a little more than usual, were sad. He was sad, his eyes that no longer reflected the cosmic madness he sought in the starry belly of Azathoth were sad. "I can't put that in my book," he told me. Bill scratched his nose and looked on.

"I just can't," Neal said. "It was just too much, you know. The little kids. They'd torn themselves to pieces, but you know a few of them tried to keep up their lessons.

They did sums on the chalkboard. One of the little boys died with *Huck Finn* in his hand. His fingers were so stiff, his little toothpick hands.... He was worried about a quiz, I could tell, because his little forehead was all furrowed like a scholar. How can I trivialize all this just by making it a story. They'd never understand," he said and he fell to his knees and wept hard toddler tears. I put a hand on his shoulder and waited, watching his long shadow sneak under my feet. Bill had left and then drove back up with a car, a great old Packard. He had our rucksacks too, in the front seat. The car idled and Neal knelt amidst the leaded smoke.

"They danced you know, the mayor did, and so did the sheriff and the pediatrician. Some kid drew that on the chalkboard too, the three of them dancing while baby stick figures cried and screamed." He looked up at me, his eyes large and star-crazed again. "The sheriff had on a cowboy hat and wore a crooked star over half his stick-line body, and they drew the doctor with a big old mirror on the top of his head, like in the movies. And they were smiling, those three characters, big crescent smiles that punched through the sides of their circle faces. But you know, it wasn't because of the pain. Cthulhu, He knows nothing of pain, or human suffering. Not any more than we know of bacterial suffering. Do they scream when we go to a doctor and take a pill? Oh, his servants danced all right, not because they loved the pain or were celebrating death, but just because not one of those poor men had ever heard so many kids scream for so long before."

Neal stood up and dusted off his knees, and then sneezed. Without a word he got into the back seat of the car and pulled our rucksacks back with him so I'd have to sit in the front with Bill, shotgun.

"Where are we headed?" I asked Bill.

Bill didn't even look at me as he shifted and stepped on the gas. "New York. We have to save the world. Only Beats and grifters and bums and junkies are immune to the Call." New York, oh how I missed her, but couldn't bear to even dream what might be happening in her valley streets. I closed my eyes and tried to extinguish the self, so that I could act without thought, but Neal shattered my arrogant meditation.

"They danced, not because they were taken over by dime-novel demons who love to listen to people suffer," he said, finally able to talk again. "They danced because the tiny bit of their brains that remained human wanted everyone to be happy and everything to be normal. And that little human bit of the brain just told their bodies that the kids were singing and would be happy if they danced, so they did."

Chapter Eight

Once, in Northport. I found myself down by the water, walking through the flat old park. I'd like to sit on a bench, shake a hand or two, and maybe wait for someone to invite me in for a drink or for a night of bracing conversation. There were some cool artists in Northport—it was close enough to Manhattan, but the houses were large and cheap, good space for studios, so painters were drawn to the little burg. Me, I was drawn to the water (this was long before I knew what horrors waited for us all in the depths of the salty seas) and to the men who worked it for their daily bread.

One guy, a round little man, the kind of joe you'd say was built like a fireplug if you thought fireplugs were a lot thicker around than they really are, was an ace with a net and a rowboat. George never failed to drag in a net full of porgies or blues, even when the other fishermen would just stare at their feet and swing empty buckets as they walked through the park and up the hill to their little homes. And George's fish were peaceful; they'd try to breathe the poison air, huffing and staring from within the lattice of his old net, but they never flopped or twitched. They were coming home, they knew.

George would clean his fish right on the shore, scaling them but never hacking off the heads or tails, while flies circled him and his catch like black snow. There's more than one unsold painting of him tucked into racks in Northport attics. The artists would wait, along with the flies, for the first traces of a red-streaked sunset, because they knew that that was when George would be coming home.

Mostly I just watched George scale, gut and sometimes fillet his fish right on the spot. He was a swordmaster with his sharp knife, black with age with a worn wooden handle. He could scale a fish in two strokes, gut it in one, and then take just an extra second to cut it into filets or steaks. Nobody could touch him for speed or grace, neither machine nor dancer could do George one better. The painters never even bothered trying to capture his real speed on canvas, instead they just went abstract on him—George's head floating above a swirl of red rain, a great white streak cutting through the sky, or just the park at dusk, George-shaped hole where he had been standing, and nothing but flies and fishguts littering the damp grass at the bottom of the canvas.

With the first fish, George would always cut out the sweetest meat and throw it away. "Leave something for the flies," he explained to me, or if I was sitting too far away, to nobody but the flies themselves. "Go on, eat your own," he'd tell them as he pulled another thick bluefish from his net, but they just kept swarming and buzzing, smacking into his head or hands, or landing on his shoulders. I swallowed more than one big horsefly myself that summer.

"You like fish?" George would ask, and I would offer to pay him, but he'd just hand me fresh-gutted fish wrapped in newspaper and wink at me, because he knew I was watching him the way I'd listen to jazz, with a heart full of love and desire. He never seemed to remember that sure, I do like fish, especially the porgies grilled still in the skin. Memere would take off the heads and tails for us first.

Three days went by and there was no George. On the first day, the painters stayed till the sun sank into the sound waiting for him to come in, but he'd never been out that day. On the second day, fewer people came, and fewer flies too. On the third day, it was just me, waiting for George, drinking a beer out of a paper bag while on my little park bench a few yards from the pier, but I didn't see him until I decided to head for home by way of the bar. He was inside, working a cat's cradle with thin white wire.

"Look, Jack," he told me. It was the first sentence I'd ever heard him say that didn't talk about fish. "Look at this." His voice was deep and dead. And George shook the wire from his fingers and into my outstretched palm. The wire was… soft. Like nylon, it was nylon, a strand thinner and tougher than I'd ever seen.

"That," George said, nodding to the mess of twists and knots in my hand, "is the future. I retire now. They'll make nets from that stuff one day, nets five miles long, and they clean the sound from Montauk to Brooklyn." I snorted, too dazed to comprehend him—I thought poor George was joking till he slammed a fist against a table. "No!" he shouted, and damn sure if his voice was the only one left in the bar, or even the town. "They will! The oceans will be lined with huge nets, they'll drift on the currents and sweep up all life. The tuna, the shark, jellyfish, porpoises… WHALES!" Some dumb drunk tittered way in the back of the room, but George didn't even have to turn around to shut him up. George inhaled sharply, and the heckler swallowed the rest of his giggling.

"Fishing, it's not an art anymore," he said. "It's war. It's the gas hissing into the showers at Auschwitz."

It was war. It's war now. There was a drift net, just like the one George told me about those years ago, ethereal and rising from the Pacific, dragging its way across America. Whole towns were falling into its haunted tangles, the souls of their resident fools the catch of the day. And me and Neal and now Bill, all piled into a Caddy Neal found parked in Goodland's local Methodist Church, were trying desperately to outrace the tide. We'd be ahead in one town, then stop for the night under a cracking moon, and in dreams I could see the dark strands drift across the night, taking whatever little town we were holed up in with it. In the morning, mugwumps ruled and the air tasted of salt and scales.

We learned to drive at night, and to head only to the cities, where there were nooks and crannies to hide in, bars a human being could still get a drink at. We moved under ground, through sewers and into basement pads with those few people, usually dharma bums and older Beats, or wild women with ironed hair, who knew enough to resist or dodge Cthulhu's inexorable reach.

Tramps and hobos poured into the cities behind us, trembling with stories of life on the road and rails. Great beasts twenty feet long were strapped down to flatbeds and screaming their way across the country, the beetlemen drivers happy to rip off and consume their own ears just so they wouldn't have to hear the wailing, wailing that could kill a man. Wheat fields burned under waves of green fire; it was cold and flowed like heavy ocean water, and left no smoke behind. "You don't burn up in it," one fellow told me, "you drown in it." He'd seen his woman go down under a wave of the stuff, and then come up, green spurting from her nose and mouth; then she went down again. "I waited for her to come up again, you know, because you're not a goner 'til you go down three times in normal water, but with this stuff you don't get no second chances." Then he cried until Neal's new girl for whatever that town we were in, Mandy or something, took him to a couch and fed him jelly-jar wine 'til he was able to sleep.

Driving was insane. Neal never slept anymore, and always wanted the wheel. He drove is in a wild route—up to Omaha for a horrible afternoon tour of a city in flames, then he pulled a massive u-turn, smoking the back wheels nearly off the back of the car, and sent us hurtling back towards Springfield. Bill was mostly on the nod—though I could never catch him making the connection, he always found his horse, no matter what lonely highway we were traveling down—so I'd have to wrestle Neal for the wheel one-on-one. I was slower than he was, and he knew the tricks of prison infighting: the knee to the balls was just a feint, I'd jerk away and right into where his thumb was waiting for my throat—but I learned a few tricks from the sutra Kilaya left me with, and sometimes I could grab that thumb and bring Neal to his knees, then start heading East again, back onto Route 66. And in the back seat, halfway between dreamland and pipe dream, Bill would mumble and prophesize of the horrors that awaited in New York. Men transformed as they strolled down the street, then scuttled up buildings with their new claws, or the tentacles with a thousand kissing suction cups, and there nested and bred for the new Reich. Babies born hideously deformed, they shattered mama's hips on the way out, all head and horns plopped atop corpse bodies. Bill called them the lucky ones.

The unlucky ones were still men and women, still normal. Far too normal, square as houses. What could they do but keep their heads down and pretend that their bosses hadn't been driven mad, and hadn't demanded that the mail room boys take off their foreskins with the sharp rocks he brought in from his driveway back in Westchester County? Cuddle up to the beetleman in bed next to you once a week? Sure, as long as he brought home his paycheck and a bag full of groceries. Better to close your girly little eyes and think of John Fitzgerald Kennedy while every hole in your body was probed by chitinous appendages, while the clicking laughter of the beast that was once your high school sweetheart ground into your ears like street glass.

New York, New York, a town so cool they damned it twice. The cult was strongest there; when Cthulhu awoke, the tidal wave of fear and change he burst forth from rose high over this land and finally broke over the purple, smog-choked sky of midnight Manhattan. Black rain fell like blessings, and coated the concrete and glass steel mountains of the haunted isle. Wall Street was ankle-deep in blood, Central Park a range where the livestock was all one succulent meat, all long pig. Get a job patrolling the border with a sharpened stick, why not? Better them than you, and besides, you got to sleep in the lobby of the Plaza Hotel, away from the smell of horse shit from the fancy hansom cabs and the sound of bones crunching under the jaws of mile-long trains of maggots.

"Just settle in for the ride, boys," Bill would mutter to us in the back seat, as I wrestled Neal for the wheel, but he wasn't talking to us, he was talking to the poor old New Yorkers who had bowed before the Dreamer, and let Him put the blinders on their souls.

In St. Louis the Cadillac gave up the ghost. We left it on the street and walked three abreast right down Perhsing Avenue. Bill was alert for a change, though his face still twitched—he blinked rapidly like a boy made slow from too much self-abuse. I almost didn't believe him when he nodded at some scorched-out ruin and said, "I was born there." Neal was strangely quiet; he kept peering up at the sky, watching the stars only he could see. We walked past the old John Burroughs school, then turned onto Price Road. "My folks have a little place up here," Bill said.

It was a damn mansion on five acres. Neal didn't even look at it, he just kept his neck craned towards the sky and twitched whenever I asked him something. The house had been trashed; a hobo jungle reined within. Steel drums littered the lobby and the roof above dripped soot like the night sky did these days. There were bottles all over the floor, and most were empty. I had to kick over seven before I found one with a little canned heat left. It was cold in the house, colder than it should have been for a sultry August evening. The drift net was passing overhead, making sure every last little guppy of a man was captured and made ready for the soul-killing knives of mugwumps. We weren't escaping, I realized. We were just being gutted and tossed aside, for the flies.

Burroughs's home was a bit of a lightning rod for every hep cat and grifter in town now. They had their stories and their battle scars (missing ears, black tongues from speaking the profane words they once overheard, eyelids sliced open with straight razors just so a body wouldn't be scooped up in his sleep), and not much more left. They didn't laugh anymore, and I missed the old lungs full of guffaws and corny old jokes. They just lay around the rooms among the cracked-up furniture, pissing and snorting and sometimes just grabbing for anyone new, someone who hadn't heard their stories a hundred times before. And we were new, so we got an earful. There was this cat named Chinese Charlie—he wasn't Chinese, but he'd been to Hong Kong and spent six months there before stowing his way home—and he told me about this girl he saw walking down a country road, her breasts big and hanging out of her nightgown. "I'm no raper of women," he told me, and his voice was painted with cheap rum and loathing, "but these days it seems I'm the only one. So I walked up to this girl, not because she was a stack of hotcakes, but because she was lost in a daze, just walking down the side of the road with her arms out to her sides, like a flying Wallenda on a circus tightrope, but I walked up to this girl see, and on her breasts she had faces! Little baby faces, like the stillborns' heads in formaldehyde jars!" Chinese Charlie was so earnest and solemn about it, laying there in the corner of the room, I just had to laugh. I cracked up like that was the funniest punchline I'd ever heard in my whole life, and the great dining room shook with my laughter.

"Oh Lord, did you get a look at what her real face looked like? Was there a family resemblence?" I asked him. Chinese Charlie frowned at me and poked a big sausage finger right in my chest. "You're cruel, you know that? You're a cruel man. Selfish and uncaring. The world is falling into the shitter, and you're here, taking some primrose path. Kickin' back. Traveling, not living. Kitchen gets too hot, you're the first one out the door. Think of that poor girl for one minute! What's she gonna feed those babies if her tits are the babies? You gonna marry that girl? Gonna give her a home and spending money for formula and food to keep those babies strong? Or are you just gonna lay her, and then tomcat right out the door into the dark of the night? She's eatin' for three, damn you!" With that Chinese Charlie folded his arms across his chest, tucked his chin in and rolled over, his back to me. All the rest of the men in the joint did that too, each turning away from me in turn. Some of them turned smartly like soldiers, others just swayed, or sat and stared right through me. I had gotten what I wanted, finally, to be left alone. No longer a shining star, not the swirling center of every big time. It wasn't all it was cracked up to be, so I ran off to find Neal, and I did, out back.

Out back was a huge expanse of blasted prairie. White wheat, smacked flat against the earth, crunched under my feet. Neal was easy to find, he was sticking right up and gesturing at the sky, and two girls were sitting on either side of him. Both of them were thin little things, thinner than he liked usually, with long ironed hair, one a dirty blonde, the other with glasses and hair like bootblack. They turned when they heard me but Neal didn't. He kept his back to me, one hand on his hip and the left outstretched towards the sky. He knew me though and said "Hi Jack, look!" And I looked right over his shoulder and at his hand. His forefinger and thumb were crooked to look like the letter C, and I looked through them (the moon wasn't bright, but I could see starlight glinting in his fingernails) and saw a star.

"So, which one of the stars on Orion's belt do you want to see me put out? Huh? Don't believe me? I can see you frowning, I have eyes in the back of my head." He laughed and the girls chuckled supportively. Neal squeezed his fingers shut. Something sizzled, like a chick lighting a cigarette, but neither of them had one, and when Neal took his hand down, the star on the left end of the constellation was missing.

"Cute," I said, looking up, squinting, trying to look for the tendril of cloud obscuring the star, but there was nothing. The sky was empty of anything but tiny white stars—even the tentacles, the wrathful face of Cthulhu and his burning moon-eye, were all gone. Just like that little star. It didn't twinkle, it was gone.

"I put out a star. A few are missing, do you notice them, or, heh heh, do you notice *not* them? There's a little poem for ya. Ever do astronomy in Boy Scouts, Jack?" Neal asked. I looked down, and the girl with the boot-black hair looked up at me and said, "It's true. Look at the Big Dipper." I couldn't bear to crane my neck up that high; I just did not want to see what Neal was doing to the sky. "You're going off the deep end," I told him. "Listen. Don't you remember the kids?"

"Oh yeah. Yeah, the kids," he said, and he squeezed his fingers shut again, just like snuffing out a candle. "Poor kids, poor old things, but there's no free ride out here, you know. The wheel just keeps on turning, and if in this life you don't get a chance to fall into bed with a belly full of beer and a lovely girl, then maybe in the next, you know. Got to look at the big picture, the big paint-splattered action painting." He turned to me, "The universe is a Jackson Pollock. I guess we're all just a bunch of drips and...!" he said, and then the nervous heh heh hehs of Neal's craziness ate the rest of his sentence. He turned back to the sky and went back to putting out stars.

Back inside I stepped over tangled messes of tramps and musicians with scraggly beards, kicking past comic books and bongo drums and empty bottles, and took up the steps to find Bill. He was up in his boyhood bedroom, sitting on the side of the bed like a bus was about to pull in and take him downtown to the Woolworth's, reading a little pulp digest. He looked up at me with his wide and tired eyes, went "Hmph" and then turned back to his magazine.

"Neal is putting out the stars. He holds his fingers up and crushes the life out of them right up there in the sky. I stared at where one used to be; it wasn't twinkling. He's doing it."

"Impossible," Bill muttered. He licked his finger and turned the page.

"No, it isn't! I saw it…."

"Co-in-ci-DENCE!" he barked. Bill finally set aside his magazine, leaving it open face down like a tent so he could get back to the short story he was reading. I saw the cover. Something named *Super Science Stories*, it was yellowed and dog-eared (like Bill himself, already, his habit having stolen life's best years) with a pin-up girl, naked except for a green sheet, on the cover. Lightning spilled from her fingertips and above her: a city-sized foo fighter drifted in space. "Look, there's no way, no matter what powers Neal may be making Faustian bargains with. Stars are light-years away, sometimes thousands of light-years away. The sky you see tonight died an aeon ago. We're just late in getting the news, is all." He pulled himself across the bed to the little window and parted the curtain. "What's missing?" he asked.

"The left star on Orion's belt. If you look over…."

"I know where it is!" He peered up through the window, licked his palm and smeared the dust on the glass with it to get a better look. "Alnitak, I think. Yep, not there anymore." He turned back to me. "Eight hundred years ago, that star sniffed itself out, not tonight. We just figured out that it was lost this evening. The star was dead by the time it was named. Didn't you ever have a telescope as a kid, Jackie?" he asked. Bill rose, like an old man, and in a step was across the room and kneeling in front of a two-shelf bookcase painted in a gay red. He pulled another little paperback out from it and flipped through the pages, wetting his thumb each time. "The belt of al-Jauza," Bill chuckled, "al-Jauza," he said again, and then another time. "Sort of… the central female. I should have paid more attention when I was in Tangiers."

He looked up at me. Bill had that sallow yellow skin, still. I wonder if he had actually just been this way as a boy too, stuck in a tiny room on top of a mansion, playing with fantasies of star charts and bug-eyed monsters, and shooting little birds with his Daisy air rifle. I almost asked him, but I didn't care that much, and the old bull was on a roll.

"Mother Space! That's a kick, ain't it? The woman at the center of the cosmos, upon which all creation revolves, and Neal is trying to get her to drop her knickers. Man, some fellas never change." Bill pushed out his leg and wormed back up onto the bed, then got on his back and picked up his magazine, holding it far from his face. It was a weird pose, a way to tell me to leave and go downstairs and see if there was enough beer in the Frigidaire.

I was halfway through the door when Bill cleared his throat, the soft machines in his throat and chest clanking and grinding. "You know, *Jacques*," he said, "Neal could not have extinguished those stars, not in the traditional three-dimensional universe, the world of length and breadth and width that moves through time like a cosmos-shaped arrow. But if there was a higher world, think of that? Think of the universe of a black orange speckled with white all the way to the seeds, in the hands of gods who ooze through reality like gin sluicing through ice cubes in some propane salesman's after-work cocktail. If Neal could reach up and into those higher dimensions, he could extinguish the stars now, but be doing it 800 years ago. From the vantage point of those higher worlds, where even time was just a ball to juggle, Alnitak wouldn't be a massive gas giant many times larger than Sol, it would be a pinpoint, a flaming matchhead. Easy to snuff out between two fingertips bigger than galaxies. The trick would really be to only snuff out one star and not a billion of them."

Bill turned over onto his side and hugged himself. "Yeah, that would do it. Of course, if he had that kind of power I wish he'd just create a tesseract and drag New York over to us. These damn cross-country trips make me sick to my stomach. All that driving and those lonely wormy roads." The open magazine Bill put over the side of his head like it was a tent. "Turn off the light on your way out, would you? Thanks."

So that was it. I left and headed back downstairs, the tiny buzz of my own enlightenment smashed flat by the very idea of Neal. Neal, bigger than the world. Neal, who wept for kids like a man, who only needed a wheel in his hands and four on the floor to navigate the bardo; Neal, who had it all in his hands. Neal, who wasn't out back anymore, so I went through the kitchen and saw Chinese Charlie making the girl with the bootblack hair, the two of them squirming under the man's street-beaten Army overcoat. I caught a glimpse of the curve of the girl's breast—no face, just a little underripe plum of a nipple. Good for Chinese Charlie.

In the kitchen, I was alone. It was a big room with a cool tile floor under the trash, crumpled butcher paper and stains from spilled beans and slapping footprints. And there was beer. A whole palette of cans in corrugated cardboard cases, all warm. There was no ice in the Frigidaire's freezer section, but that was fine. It was cooling down quickly out on the front porch, away from the sounds of homeless moaning, and with at least the mansion between me and the dead stars missing from the sky, so I took a case out there with me and cracked open can after can. It was a game, how much beer could I get into my mouth and throat without puffing out my cheeks. After a few tries, I swallowed a whole can (minus a waterfall of foam down my shirt and slacks) of the bitter stuff in one swift and graceful chug—head back, arm up, mouth open wide, it was the sweetest inhalation.

I tried it again and again and lost the trick as the booze hit my bloodstream. I kept trying though, and let the empty cans roll from my fingers and off the porch. The earth itself tilted strangely, like a car doing ninety on a hairpin turn round a mountainside and I saw the sky. The stars were going out, slowly but surely, one at the time, like baseball players dawdling before finally leaving the field and heading back to the dugout. There wasn't a cloud in the sky, just ink peppered with sparkles, and fewer of those by the second. I drank another beer because beer was real. My tongue was already numb, so that made it easier (it was some horrible local brew, made from black river water and aged for a day or three) to just pour it down my mouth like a trough. Rough beer does a number on you right quick, drinking paint mixed with pebbles wouldn't have been much less fun, but it was numbing like it I wanted it to be. Numb like I want to be, fingers tingling and heavy against the latest can. I dropped it and booze fed the earth. Onto the second case, very heroic. Even my bones were drunk. The porch felt so good, thick paint still held the heat from the daytime, and stretched out and drifted off to sleep.

I dreamed of a raft on a winedark sea, bobbing slow and gentle like a kid being dandled on his grandpa's lap. The water was like quicksilver, running fast and dry over my skin and pooling in my boots and pants. It was warm out on the ocean, the damp heat of summer was a little campfire and blanket both. Then from the purple sky tentacles fell like curtains, but I was not afraid. They stroked me, fingers in my hair, over my lips in that thrilling lover's caress. The tentacles kept me warm as a chill rose from the bottom of the sea.

From ten thousand miles away I heard the screams, tinny AM radio yelps. My consciousness flew in lazy circles and dips, away from my body and towards the old mansion; it was being torn apart by space itself while robed cultists holding their torches high chanted from the curb. Space no longer defined by absence, but by presence, the presence of those familiar slithering tentacles. They weren't unfurling down from the sky, they were the sky, the space between breaths and raindrops. Like a honeybee I drifted between them, tiny and disinterested in anything but sweet ambrosia, a glistening puddle of spilled beer. Limbs and sprays of blood, splintered wood and hissing pipes flew past, but I could just buzz around them on etheric current. The tentacles were everywhere, and that isn't a description of their location, but just a fact of existence—if something existed, it was thick alien meat, stench and rubber and molten lead blood in five dimension. The world we knew was just cheap ink, flat and stretched beyond recognition against the Silly Putty surface of the REAL world. The world of the Great Dreamer, whose every somnambulant twitch and snort shook the planet and every work-a-day mind it. Except for honeybee me, my brain on a wing and a prayer.

And Bill. He burst out of his boyhood room (which was but a mass of tentacles) with a moviehouse tommy-gun and screamed about Nazis and Bombay. Stars and torchlight danced in the trap of his impossibly thick Coke bottle glasses. He lifted the gun high and with an Indian war whoop, pulled the trigger. Flames belched forth from the muzzle and bullets ripped through the air (and through the meat of the Old God's waking dream). Bill cackled as he swept back and forth with his machine gun (spent casings fell like rain, and danced on the hardwood floors) and made headway, step after painful step. Outside the mansion, some of the cultists, those old schoolmarms and clock punchers, choked on lead and fell, grinning blood.

But it wasn't. The bullets ran out before the cultists did, and Bill's hard march forward stopped, his tommy-gun's riot of poetry reduced to impotent clicking. Then the clicking of the beetlemen picked up the beat, and the drapery of tentacles returned to drown him and all the other riffraff in the Burroughs manse. He went down beneath undulating black waves, his fist clenched and veined like marble.

Then Neal, nine hundred feet tall and glowing with St. Elmo's fire, parted the curtain and smiled. A kid peeking to watch a girl roll down her stockings and then, after an eternity, unsnap her bra, that was Neal's smile. And as easy as a boy pushing curtains aside, he saved the world. The Dreamer Of The Deep was pushed aside with a casual wave, the kind of wave Neal would offer girls as we drove past.

I woke up on the porch, my shirt stuck to the paint

thanks to sticky beer and burnt blood. Gunpowder filled the air. Most of the rest of the mansion was gone, like it had exploded, but the field and streets were utterly clear of any debris. The house blew up years ago. Nothing but an eastern wall and blasted black fireplaces topped with impotent, wilting chimneys in the distance remained. The bricks dripped a pungent slime. Bill stood right in the middle of the wreckage, smoke dancing from the barrel of his gun like he'd been smoking it. Neal was stretched across a couch, one perfectly preserved (not even cigarette burns, forget the lack of ectoplasm of scorch marks) eating from a tin of Vienna sausages. He was stabbing into it with his old pocketknife and eating the meat right off the tip of the blade.

The streets were littered with corpses, beetlemen and Beat both. I noticed the head of the girl with bootblack hair (well, her hair and the rancid meatloaf it was attached to) but everyone, everything else, had been thrown a bit too forcefully across the landscape to makes heads or tails of. They'd been just a little too sober when the psychic onslaught began. Loose shoes were everywhere. Bill walked through the doorway, the only part of the house's façade still standing after the porch, and kneeled down next to me. Behind us, we could hear a can hit the ground and Neal's chainsaw snore start up. I looked back at him. The poor guy had wet himself during the night.

"He's going to betray you, you know," Bill told me, his voice an aria wrapped in a bull's angry snort. I looked up at him. I never liked Bill, really. He was a fag, and a rich boy, he never had to fight for anything. When the rest of us Beats were exploring the country, he ran off to Mexico, to Asia, to anywhere where a boy would bend over for an American dollar and a smile. He was a junkie, his soul had been eaten away years before R'lyeh rose in the roiling Pacific. But I respected him, because he was a survivor, a roach like the mugwumps. When Neal and I were dust, William S. Burroughs would still be kicking around (hell, the bastard would still be writing for publication; I already shot my load with that) so I didn't punch him in the face right then and there. Anybody else I would have, even Neal; if he came to me and said "I'm going to betray you, you know. Tie you to an obsidian slab and draw your heart out through your nostril, just to make Cthulhu chuckle," he would have gotten a faceful of knuckles. Not Bill though. I didn't like him. But I respected him.

"It's pulp fiction. Neal's not on our side, he's on his side. Against the Dreamer, but not against the starry wisdom Azathoth teased him with."

"How do you know?"

He snorted again (it was dusty without a house to protect us from the wind kicking through the ruined wheat). "I read magazines. You two were best friends once, but now, years later, you're just going through the motions. Two dreamers chasing dreams. He's married—when he's not balling girls two at a time while we stand guard, he's playing house with some heifer and teaching his rugrats how to pray, hands all steepled together at the side of the bed." (Bill almost got a punch there too, but I was too drained to move.) "And you… Christ, Jack. You know your problems. This spiral path only has one ending. Of course he has to betray you, and by doing so, betray us all. It's *The Shadow.* Neal's the butler, and the butler did it. That's the goddamn ending to the novel he's writing about this! Pure pulp fiction."

He plopped down and tucked his legs under his ass like a kid. "Eh, fuck it, Jack. Neal would be crossing you over a pussy if he wasn't going to cross you over the whole goddamn ball of mud. Fuckin' world half deserves it anyway, as far as I can tell."

"Yeah, so why you'd come save us back in Kansas, hmm?" He wasn't looking at me, so I could lick beer off the plank in front of me (the smell had been driving me up the wall) and listen to him answer at the same time. I didn't want to look at Bill. He looked so old, like a snake skin left behind.

"I told you already," he croaked, "there's only one ending to this. You and Neal ain't the only ones with a taste of enlightenment. A dragon came to me, after decades of chasing it, and told me what needed doing. You know, I'm going to move to Kansas one day."

"Wow."

"I'm not looking forward to it either."

For a long time we did nothing but listen to Neal snore. "So…."

Bill finally turned to me, his eyes a squint. "How are your sales?"

And I laughed. I roared like the damn King of England after the court jester shits himself. "Damn! Royalties! Is that all you can think of?" He wasn't joking, but I loved the man's punchline. I laughed more and more, just jiggling on the porch; it crippled me.

"Real good. Haven't had to write another word, really."

"Yeah. The ban's off my book now. It's doing well. Thanks for the title by the way." Then we heard Neal stir and stopped talking about books. Neither of us were in the mood for any of Neal's theories of literature now and I wasn't interested in hearing about how this would make yet another thrilling chapter. He spilled off the couch and hopped up onto he porch (ignoring the skeletal doorway that still stood) and stretched his arms out, a farm boy taking in the view of the north forty.

"Woo! I tell ya boys, this is what happens when we stick our heads up above ground. We got to be gophers from now on. Or mole people! Just like in those old serials. We'll come up at night, for provisions and women in pillbox hats and bullet bras. They'll hold their little hands to their cheeks and screech when they see us, but gemstone tiaras and princess gowns will make 'em ours again, right, my mole brothers?" Then he laughed at his joke, alone.

"Let's find a new car," Bill said and we were off. The neighborhood was deserted. Doors flapped open and shut in the wind, little stores all ready for customers with the blinds pulled up and display cases shiny, but not a man was about. No squirrels either, and the sky (only blue streaked with the sharpest of purple clouds and the occasional stream of a moon rocket heading off the marble) was free of birds and bugs. And damnit if every car we came across wasn't a burnt-out husk.

"This is getting repetitive," Neal said, as we stumbled across the second used car lot with nothing but smoldering hunks on display or in the windows. "Aren't there any good ghosts in this country? Or is every inch of the way going to be madmen and spirits from the fifth dimension?"

Good ghosts. That reminded me, there were good ghosts. Spirits summoned by bebop and cooked up in sweet whisky. Called by blood, but not blood tainted by human fear and madness, but the good blood that spilled from food and fed the earth. The world was still drenched in the spirit of the Lord, and his little children, the wayward ones who never left their childish things behind, they were the ones set to inherit the earth, if only we could end the reign of the cult. So I summoned one, the good old-fashioned way. I walked to the other side of the street, where the traffic would have headed east had there been any, and stuck out my thumb.

Bill and Neal stayed on the other side of the highway and just looked at me. A pair of yokels taking in the real live genuine article. King of the Beats. Looking to hitch. On the road again.

And the car pulled up, an old model Cadillac—pre-war it looked like, all curves but for the creased hood up front. It looked familiar, and then it pulled up. It was a Sedan by Tiffany's—glass spun and blown, translucent but without motor or works, and I was in the passenger seat already. A younger me, baby eyelids fluttering in sleep. Jack Kerouac, minus a decade and change, and a thousand gallons of cheap alcohol, the years peeled off my skin as if by a potato peeler. And Neal was driving with an easy smile and only a wrist on the wheel. He was young too, nose not so red yet, hair full and black, not pasted down over his receding hairline. Our paunches were missing.

"So, you two fine upstanding American citizens need a lift anywhere in particular?" ghostly Neal asked me. Bill and the real Neal cut across the street quick like bunnies to take in the car. The one we had already driven in, the one with the cracked leather dash from the New Orleans heat and the Colorado altitude (but this dash was smooth as mirrors).

"We actually need the car," Bill said, and he grabbed for the door handle but his hand passed right through it. "Neal!" Neal said, sliding his butt up onto the hood. "Care to know who wins the third race in St. Louis twelve years after your trip? Write it down, make sure you're here on the day, and you can double your life-savings. It's all scientific, like the theory of relativity. You've been driving so fast you caught up with yourself."

Ghostly Neal laughed. "And all you want is a car, eh?" He nudged my doppelganger, who awoke with a slow-motion start. "Sounds like a good deal to me. Can't beat the scientific method, and I'm sure Sal and I can ride the rails, and dream some dreams of our own."

My Neal smiled and just told him, "Childhood's End, guaranteed." Neal in the car ducked down and found a pencil and scrap of paper, wrote down the name and tucked the scrap in his shoe. He just stood up and walked through the car. Young Jack opened the door and stumbled out, yawning fiercely and with a fist in his eye to drive away the sleep. "Whuzzat?" I said, brilliantly.

The car was solid, and ours, and drove like we were three inches over the road, which we probably were. I waved to my ghost, but he was too busy rubbing his face to wave back. Young Neal whooped and waved, and we all (even surly Bill in the now solid backseat, his other hand over his nauseous stomach) waved back. Bill turned, "Nice trick, getting your own car from yourself."

"Yeah, and it probably never needs gas! Hey Neal, how did you know what horse was going to win? Or was it just grift?"

"Nope, honest injun, Childhood's End is going to win. Neal ain't though. That was yesterday's race, and we were too busy moving into William's abode yesterday to get down to the track. And the phone was disconnected, so I couldn't place any bets from the house." He looked into the rear-view mirror and addressed the back seat. " For a bunch of Richie Riches, your family sure knows how to be inconveniently delinquent with the phone company. Don't you know that International Telephone and Telegraph takes no prisoners? Ma Bell!" he shouted and stepped on the gas hard, taking the wind out of us passengers. We ate Missouri for breakfast in the American dream car.

"Yeah, but how did you know?" I asked Neal again later when we were idling and Bill was off pissing in the trees off the side of the highway. "Enlightenment for worldly trivia is a blasphemous thing."

Neal just kicked off his old stitched rag of a shoe, leaned down and pulled a wrinkled scrap of paper from the toe. He smoothed it between his fingers and held it out for me to read. Under the smear of lead, I could just barely make it out: Childhood's End. "That's why I always wanted to drive, brother. I didn't want to get here too late. But I guess I did." Then Neal dropped the paper and let the wind take it as he walked off into the trees and started to piss as well. I leaned back on the wheel well and put my palms back against the purring hood of the car. Even running at an idle in the afternoon heat of Missouri, the steel of my past was cool to the touch.

Chapter Nine

Great Chicago glowed red before our eyes. We were suddenly on Madison Street among hordes of cultists, some of them sprawled out on the street, elongated chitinous scythes where their hands used to be dragging across the ground, hundreds of others gathered around storefront churches or crowded onto corners, all waiting and buzzing. "Wup! Wup! Neal approaches! The Man Of Two Worlds, chosen one of Azathoth! All hail Neal!" I cut the wheel hard and proceeded to downtown Chicago, but there wasn't a true human on the streets anymore. Only mockeries of life: flatulent mugwumps in clouds of swampgas, children oozing along the streets on a mass of thick cilia, hawking newspapers of human skin scrawled with unspeakable blasphemies, letters you couldn't even trace upon a page without the madness coming for you. And those were the remnants of our sweet race, the folks who were people once before R'lyeh rose and the missiles tore their way up from the deserts—there were plenty of pretty girls with a smile for our dream car and swarthy working stiffs, chests broad as barrels and v-shaped torsos leading to chinos and black boots, but there were not women, they were not women, they were not men.

Shoggoths to a being they were, phalanges, avatars of insanity and destruction mocking me with human form and countenance.

Finally, I pulled over at the YMCA. Old Bull's childhood piggybank would pay for a night or two. The Cadillac I pointed snout out and ready to go, nobody parallel parked anymore. It was the little things I noticed. The peculiar half-East, half-West of Chicago was only subtly warped by the shoggoth population. "Potatoheads," Bill muttered to me, while Neal ran off to the corner to talk to one, a middle-aged colored woman with swinging hips. They embraced quickly, like veterans, patting each other on the back, and walked off without Neal even saying goodbye.

Bill's old coins weren't marked with the Elder Sign, either the thin branch or the burning five-pointed star with that great fried-egg-eye in the middle of it, so we weren't going to be getting a room. The car of American dreams had conveniently faded back to the ether and mother Earth quaked again, stretching and cracking the city's streets in every direction. Bill stood all hunched up, wearing his suit like he was a child trying on papa's clothes, fabric pooled around his shoulders, wrists and ankles. What an unclean little man he was; I just felt the urge to punch him, just to see the slime bubble and splurt out of his earholes. But instead I told him of how last time when I was here with Neal, when our Cadillac was a steel prophet and not a speedy phantasm, we listened to bebop and on the intermissions would growl down the streets in our car until God showed up.

"George Shearing, giant old egghead. A master of the ivories. Every stroke a completed action, a day in the life of a tragic hero. You know, Bill? God. Last time I was in Chicago, I was in the very same room with God."

"I see God right now," Bill said, his eyebrows up, and I turned around to see Cyclopean modern towers and pinnacles rising flowerlike and delicate like spun crystal to reach for the black and deadly sky. No Cthulhu, none of the swirling red stars of Azathoth mocking us from the heavens, just black. The stars were all dead as coal, the moon blasted to less than dust by the thunder of rockets. And silence. The weird ululations of the city's ruckus fell to a whisper, and then into nothingness. Mother Earth inhaled again, and her fecund bulk shifted, tenderly like Memere brushing my bangs from my eyes as a little boy. And there was God in that blasted night, the God of oblivion where even the horrid clash of pincers, scales and flailing tentacles fade to the wonder of nothingness.

"Kireji!" I cried out desperately. My word didn't echo across the curving alleys or the passages lined with red Gregorian brick, buildings designed to weather winter's hammer, but which seemed like naught but gilded futility to me. We were alone in this universe, a wonder that came to me all at once as I saw the God Bill saw. God is the absence of this all, of us all. "Kireji!" I shouted again, and the furious exhalation died just past my lips. Kireji, that decisive moment in the haiku, where one syllable betrays a thought, a shift in the breath, the contemplation of time and nature without emotion; but nature was too foul and dark. Even God had turned His head away from us, away from *ti jean* when I needed Him most.

If I had all the paper on the earth, I couldn't express what I saw that night, but seventeen syllables of haiku, perhaps that would have been too much. "For now we see through a glass, darkly; but then face to face," I said to myself (could Bill even hear me; I felt Great Mother still slowly exhaling, the curve of the earth swelling and drawing me up towards the sky). "Now I know." I didn't finish the verse. I did know, because I was staring up at the dark glass of the Chicago night.

This was supposed to be some kind of drama. I'd been given just enough information to get by, thanks to little buzzes in my ear by the demon Kilaya, my sweet and pure Marie. Neal showed up just in time; so did Allen and so did Bill. Hell, so did the old bums and the bennies and the truckers and cool bottles of Coke for sale on the side of the highway by some round peach of an old lady with flabby arms and a wrinkly smile. We may well have been immune to the siren call of the cult; our features were still men's features, our profiles human, but we were being pushed and shoved around, like a kid making an inch worm crawl down some specific twig and onto a particular leaf that just happens to be square on the bottom of a crystal-clear Mason jar. The sky was clear that night too.

"See," Bill said. "There's Neal!" Then he cackled, his laugh wet and nasty. He was just happy to be out of the damn car.

Neal was heading back our way, an entourage of cheering cultists and hobos, all drunk and stuffed to the gills with Vienna Beef, behind him. Trudging quietly amidst the group was this little Mexican girl, walking like she was on her way to First Communion.

Neal hugged me hard (he was flabby just a few minutes ago, now his arms were like steel cables twisted around granite bones) and said, "You're standing up for me, Jack! I'm getting married tonight! It'll be a great little scene for my book. Marriage, a night alone with my little girl in a little Chicago railroad apartment, the el chugging away outside—I'll leave out the bit about the trains being nothing but giant white worms snaking across the city like the tracks were garden paths—making sweet love before heading out to that final battle with lords dark and sundry, with two boon companions at my side. A sure-fire bestseller, don't you think."

Bill said, "I like it, but I don't think Jack reads adventure books. You'll probably just lose him in the story. It's not so stream-of-consciousness if you go out of your way to get married just to shoehorn in a sex scene, is it Jack?"

"I'm hungry," I said. "Do any of your friends have that tainted money people in this town want?" I don't think we had eaten in days, and I was drying out from the beer and the race down the highways to Chicago. The whole town smelled of beef to me; I would have eaten a brick if it had gravy on it.

"A wedding feast! Perfect idea, we were just on our way." Behind Neal, the shoggoths tittered and nodded. I squinted at the girl; she was a young one, not more than fifteen, with eyes so brown you couldn't see where pupil ended and iris began half the time—a lesser man, or a better man, really, would have looked away from her solemn stare, but I'd just seen God. A pair of kewpie doll eyes weren't going to do it anymore, even if planted on a sweet bronze apple of a face, one framed with straight black hair, the kind that just falls over shoulders and down backs without ironing or clouds of noxious spray—she had that hair of least resistance. Cute little thing, just grist for Neal's mill. She didn't stare back at me or flinch and look down like a lot of Neal's pick-ups in the old days used to, she just looked right through me, disinterested.

The rest of the gang were simultaneously well- and poorly dressed; they wore fine suits and skirts probably snatched right off store window dummies. Some wore thick scarves even in the heat of late July, and not in the fashion of some hip young girl struggling to look continental either. They had the vague facial features of shoggoths now. I'd seen enough of them now; even when they mocked human forms, they never did it perfectly. Hooked noses, goggle-eyes, receded chins like some inbred British royal. I didn't need my third eye to see their auras; the degraded sham of creation was obvious to any sharp observer. They marched down the middle of the empty street, right down the yellow lines, with me and Bill in the middle of the circle, taking up right behind Neal and his latest little thing.

"This is really queer," I told Bill, talking between my teeth. It's not like they couldn't hear me, but I felt like an infantryman being led to some POW camp, and found myself playing the part.

"Ah you get used to it," he grumbled. He made me mad. Bill had a pistol jammed into his pants again too, probably part of what was weighing them down. A two-bit fag gangster; of course he didn't care so much about the beetlemen, they may as well have run off the pages of his own damn book. I glanced over at Neal; he was nearly skipping, his hand swinging with his girl's. A young man again. Even Chicago was against me, dead and not rowdy, quiet except for wet soles slapping on asphalt, not one fat Polack screaming down the street, no bakeries puffing out after-hour clouds of the sweet smell of newborn bread.

Not one of the female shoggoths was remotely makeable, though they tried. The dimensions were just off—one looked like she had an ottoman stuffed under the back of her skirt, another a bust that was half-busted at least. We walked a few blocks before finding some VFW hall in a storefront of a rundown little rowhouse that was twisted enough that its right side had five stories and its left side only four. Neal jimmied the lock and pushed the door wide open, crying, "Hallelujah! The time has come for me to take a bride!" He spun and wiggled his eyebrows. "So, where do you think I should take her first?" Then he danced inside, limbs loose like the old Neal. The party kicked up the second he entered the room. Table settings for a hundred, with the big table for the wedding party empty (Bill sat next to me like we were going to have to dance together, usher and bridesmaid) but every other seat already jammed with some hideous monster or bloated account executive with wine-red cheeks. They all gibbered identically though, the slimy purple fellows with no mouths but for fleshy orifices that squeezed open and shut like sphincters, and the two brothers with electric plaid jackets who co-owned the Greater Maywood Pre-Owned Ford and could make even a goblin a sweet deal on a pre-war creampuff. Yes, they gibbered louder than even skittering mechano-roaches who crunched whole bowls of shrimp scampi down their ravenous gullets while scampering about the tables and knocking over centerpieces. It was a real peach of a wedding party, with multi-colored crepe paper streamers and flowers with living razors for petals clicking in piles in each corner.

A foul wind blew the door open and a shadow dark as coal slid in and over the polished wood floor. With it came a blanket of silence, even Jimmy and Jerry (the fellows with the car lot) clammed up finally. And the shadow trembled, then erupted into a pillar that hit the ceiling with a furious quiet. And the shadow spoke, finally, a whisper of stone on ancient stone, in our minds. It was Dreamland's own country parson, here to pronounce Neal and skirt man and whore of Babylon. As he recited some blasted liturgy in words I couldn't understand, but that I nevertheless *knew*, the wriggling column shifted and shrank into a more human, but not a more pleasing, shape. The rhetoric was pure blasphemy, the stuff of nameless tortures and blood drunk as easily as cheap beer, but Neal just sat there with his country grin on his face, drinking it all in. Wifey was humble in the chair next to him, eyes lowered and chin tucked against her collarbone. Like vibrations on the railroad tracks it came to me; forget the blood and guts. My poor little human brain wasn't even bothering to translate a tenth of what the pastor was ranting; there was a deeper meaning to it all, the mountainous iceberg of it occulted by the deep ocean of my unconsciousness. I knew because I turned to Bill and he was white as a knucklebone, his fingers twitching, and a bit of blood drinking and carcass-rape wouldn't even get that old pervert worked up.

Preacher Horror was nearly human now; impossible wrinkled and stooped over, eyes gone and sockets nearly endless in their depth, teeth thick as gravestones and brown besides, his leer fixed since he need not speak but only think his mad gibbering blasphemies to cement this union. Limbs, only four of them now, but the vestigal stumps from his transitional tentacles still swayed with the rhythm of his cant as they sunk back into his torso.

My fevered brain filled with the black clouds of this matrimonial horror, clouding out all sense and reason. I wasn't nearly drunk enough for this; I could feel the ritual pulling me in, like the musky taste of a woman on the edge of my lips. Bill did what my muscles rebelled against doing. He pulled out his gun and fired it right at the preacher. A bullet smacked right into the forehead of the man-thing and kept right on going, not breaking the skin or shattering bone (since the beast had none, being only viscous shadows and strangled, ancient spells) at all. Instead it burrowed in and slowly stretched the back of the preacher's head, first six inches, then a foot, then two feet, the little bullet struggling to finally pierce the preacher and lead a parade of brainy goop out the back of his head. Then with a whip-crack, the back of preacher's head snapped back into place, and Neal and his girl were named man and wife with a final swampy gibber.

"Women! I love, love, love women! I think women are wonderful! I love women!" Neal cried out, and he kissed his little china doll hard. Great beads of sweat fell from his forehead from pure excitement, but the girl was placid, her mouth just a slot for tongue. A cacophony of forks started up against the glasses.

"I think I'll shoot him instead," Bill said, cranking his arm to put the barrel of his pistol at the base of Neal's busy little head, but I grabbed his wrist. "No!" I told him. "All this nonsense just proves that Neal is still the key to all this somehow."

Bill lowered the gun, but kept it right on the table next to the salad fork. Neal and his girl were still going at it, to hoots and clapping flippers, but most of the humans (or mocking man-shaped shoggoths) had turned to their bratwursts (or mocking bratwurst-shaped shoggoths; I waited for Bill to take a bite before diving in myself).

"I feel like I lost a quart of blood. Neal is a goddamn asshole, and I don't care what he thinks or what the mugwumps think. I'd want to shoot him if we weren't knee-deep in dark dimensions."

Bill ate and drank with the abandon of a junky and a hobo combined, and I followed as best I could, and danced with a few of the human-seeming girls—some were monsters, others flesh and blood, one was just a fag in drag.

Neal was a gun firing in every direction at once, as usual, leading a bunny hop, then swinging with his stonefaced but limber wifey. The music wasn't anything but the grinding of five-dimensional space against the floor of the world, but it had a beat and you could dance to it. I got tired quickly though, and leaned up against the wall to watch Neal. He was flailing his arms, cutting from one partner to another, kissing other girls while the little Mexican girl just looked on, standing stock still, 'til Neal touched her again and demanded some animation from her.

Clothes hit the ground with a sudden violence, and an orgy of men and monster was on—tentacles probing orifices, flesh caressed by scale and slime, fat men crawling from teat to tit and back again. Even old Bill was poking around (literally) the edges of the cluster. For a long moment I wished I had Memere's old rosary beads, but I couldn't turn my head away. Once again, I did the absurd thing and crawled into the mess myself. I didn't even need to take off my clothes. Inhuman limbs snaked under my collar and then into the waist of my pants, hungry for real American meat. I spread out my arms and legs and just floated atop the crowd; it held me aloft like I was in the Dead Sea, where the salt can keep anyone buoyant.

Of course, Neal's marriage lasted all of three days, of course of course. Bill and I were staying with some squatters, a family of Beats with a little beatnik baby even, in the sub-basement of a Greektown diner. I found myself worrying about the kid (I found myself thinking the word "rugrat") because the place wasn't well-ventilated, and if the smell of grease wasn't pushing its way down the creaky wooden steps from upstairs it was only because of the cloud of marijuana smoke that filled the place like those new Styrofoam packing peanuts. Bill spent most of his time in the corner, his ear cupped to a headset connected to a crystal radio set he found amidst the boxes. I entertained a parade of marginal sorts—fat Puerto Rican women with great pans of beans, cranky old men who still read the tattered racing forms from months ago though all the horses had been killed and eaten in lumpenprole bacchanals. The hungry, not the hip, ruled the tracks after all. I passed on the octopus salad.

"The Reds are ready to drop the big one on us," Bill said, more than once, but always calm as parking lots. The days were cool and relaxing except for the frequent parades through the streets, full of puppet-string patriotism and flags with glowing eyes amidst the field of white stars. I was standing atop a box of pre-cut French-fried potatoes, staring through the bars of the window, when I saw Neal's dancing feet heading our way. In seconds, he was down in the sub-basement with us, declaring his blasphemous annulment!

"Friends! I melted the bitch!" Neal said, smacking his hands against his chest. "She didn't last through the consummation before dissolving like a sugar-candy skull in a hot Mexican mouth, I tell you!"

"Neal, shut it, I'm trying to listen to the news. Frisco is flooding," Bill said.

Neal ignored him and hugged me hard. He lifted me six inches off the ground, a feat formerly impossible for him. "You can't stop Neal," he said right in my face. "Pow! Zoom! Gookly gooky, Neal's a spooky! Poof, I'm outta here!"

"Well," Bill said, "now that we're all here again, let's get going. The world's already all bureaucracy and flood plains; I want to put some holes in the cult already. That is what we are supposed to be doing, right?"

I didn't know what we were supposed to be doing. Neal was such an imponderable. He left me baking with a Mexican fever once and now spent half his days cavorting with the enemy and I was still ready to ride shotgun on whatever car he felt like stealing, roll right up Broadway and do who knows what to save the world from the perils of desire.

"I had tons of problems with the in-laws too," Neal said. "So many demands. They're so hungry all the time, for a little flesh, a little soul. Just last night we were atop a skyscraper, right over the flaming lake, calling up the dark forces to further bind the populace to the blind chaos of Azathoth. Out over the horizon Cthulhu was rising as well—the two don't necessarily get along, I just realized this. Earth is like a Gettysburg pebble for the two of them really, as they lead mad and bloody charges against one another. But under the ectoplasm, they are brothers, truly. I was just standing off to the side with my girl, her little hand in mine, watching the ceremony. It was like a blasphemous roller derby, boys. I don't even know what we would have ended up experiencing—the salty embrace of Cthulhu or Azathoth's swirling wisdom; but then God showed up, like a ghost."

Bill finally looked up from his radio set. I wasn't sure what to say myself. "You know, George Shearing," Neal said. "He was white as a ghost, his fingers trembling. I don't know how he got on the roof with the rest of us—I'm damn sure I would have noticed George Shearing as we all squeezed our way up the stairwells—and that spark in him was gone. God had withered on the vine. He didn't even smell like beer in the way old jazz guys tend to these days, that sweet and hollow creamy fog of beer was gone. Replaced with the sweat of illness, decay.

"The man was a pickle," Neal said, giddy. "Briny and preserved. And it struck me then, you know, just how insignificant we are. George Shearing spent his life mastering, what, a musical instrument that is only a thousand years old, for an artform that is what, fifty years old, and already half-dead, so some people who are thirty years old can be happy for an hour. And we call this mayfly tinkling God, Jack. Let me tell you, tonight I really saw God…."

"Shaddup!" Bill demanded in the corner. He was back to his radio set, a hand cupped around the headphone at his ear. "They're saying the big one hit San Fran. The Bay is reclaiming the city."

Then I knew it wasn't Neal. Not because the news didn't affect him, like it did me (I could only see Allen and his little fag friend drowning in the swiftly tilting sewers, the swinging lanterns outside Chinatown restaurants swallowed under black waves), but because he actually shut up. Neal never stopped talking on command, for anybody.

Shoggoth! The thought arced between me and the false Neal, and it showed its true colors right away. Neal didn't turn to face me, his face *shifted* to the side of his head and glared at me. Its jaw was already distending, fangs like sabers gathered up at the corners of its mouth. I did the absurd thing and dropped into my tired old three-point stance and rushed the transmogrifying beast.

It was like tackling a wave on the beach. Hard and blinding, and you, and by you I mean I, of course, ended up on the floor, soaked and stunned. Neal filled the room, I was drowning in him, flailing, gasping, spitting out mouthfuls of his liquid flesh. Bill was overwhelmed too, his ratty shoes and socks up in the air, the rest of him crumpled in the cut between floor and wall.

In the haze of ectoplasm another face formed before me. Neal again, but white and desperate, begging. His face was a mask fading into a broader darkness, a mouth of madness. Teeth the size of my head solidified about me and the flimsy mask of Neal. I heard the liquid whisper of "Help me help me Jack, they have me in New York...."

The teeth were a crushing vise, looking to push the last bit of air from my lungs. Bill's pistol floated by; I grabbed it and fired. The shock of report rippled through the ectoplasm but the bullet did nothing but drill itself, almost leisurely, through the fluid atmosphere of the shoggoth. Potatoes, a watch, Bill's crumpled hat, floated by as a pulse, a flex of plasmic muscle. I was pinned against the wall, far from Bill, who was just about as bad off as I was but skinny and shriveled (were his ribs broken) and upside-down, against the opposite wall. The teeth, arranged in two arched rows, smiled in the middle of the flux.

Absurd, absurd, do the absurd thing! It's hard not to think clearly when you see your death eight feet away, slick as tusks. I kept doing sensible things; my fingers skittered along the wall, looking for some crack or handhold, legs pumping and trying to swim, sensible and useless like pantyhose. Really, there was nothing absurd to do, once jammed up against the wall. *Except!*

Except tucked in the corner, in the little bit of the room not yet flooded with the translucent crushing flesh of the monster, was a little can with a thin spritzing wand. Bug spray. I slipped towards it, not pushing against the blob, but squeezing between the wave of Neal and the smooth basement wall. I grazed the wand with a finger, then a second. I had it, and squeezing the trigger in my fist, started pumping the spray into the gelatinous mass that had me pinned. The bug dust swirled in the suspension, filling it with a pinkish fog. For a long moment nothing happened, the pressure was still nearly unbearable, and my consciousness would have dimmed around the edges if not for the bennies I'd been chewing all afternoon. Finally, the roomful of jelly spasmed and began to shrink and scream, a quiet scream though, the scream of a room nearly out of air. The teeth crumbled into icicle shards as the ectoplasm deflated—I was draped over it like a beanbag, then finally I was on my feet squeezing the last few puffs of bug dust into the shriveling mass. And along the surface, I saw Neal's white reflection, his face tortured and tired, the Divine spark enslaved to this monster. "New York, New York" he mouthed, "Save me in New York."

"Marriage and women ain't nothing but trouble," I said. Bill scrambled to his feet—he was covered in slime.

"What did you do?"

"This," I said, holding up the canister. "The absurd thing. The unexpected. Bugspray."

"Well, it isn't that absurd," Bill said. He was wiping his slimy hands onto his slimy pants, or maybe trying to wipe the slime from his pants with his slime-coated hands. Either way, he was having a rough go of it. But he was right. "The mugwumps, beetlemen. They're all insectoid. What's so absurd about having a similar chemical weakness?" Bill pulled out a soaked hanky and tried that on his hands, then his pants, giving himself an even coating.

I was pretty moist myself.

Chapter Ten

Maybe exterminating an insectoid shoggoth with bug spray wasn't absurd. Perhaps the rational was finally beginning to reassert itself. "Or maybe," Bill said, "it's a trap. To make sure we traveled to New York. All your other cross-country trips just petered out, after all." It was absurd to travel to New York now—every face belonged to Neal. He melted in and out of the expressions of the people we hurried past, his visage slipping around the back of heads, nestling in hairdos and flowing over sweating red necks to stare at us. Sometimes he was gloating, his eyes burning with a nameless evil, other times his face was plaintive and Biblical, like some prophet watching his ancient city reduced to rubble by his angry loverboy God.

"Sympathetic magic. Sometimes it is Neal, sometimes his doppelgangers, animated by horrible marionette magics." Bill was on his back, in the train yard, speaking through raspy gasps. What was really absurd was our attempt to escape Chicago. It's just twelve hours on a flatout night run to Manhattan, but we couldn't lift a car to save our lives. Maybe it was Neal at work, his great criminal mind finally turned to the service of keeping cars where they were parked, rather than liberating them. Hangers, slide hammers, nothing worked. Some of the sweetest rides were under guard, cultists snoozing within, crumpled in the front seats, fogging up the windows. We didn't have any money for gas anyway. It was absurd, almost as absurd as trying to hop the rail with William S. Burroughs in tow.

Here is how it worked, or didn't work. A train growled up to life, and slowly squealed down the tracks. We waited behind some crates, looking for an inviting train car, and then ran for it. I matched speeds, flung myself into the gap, and scrambled onto the car. Then I turned back to see wheezing Bill, arms flailing, trying to keep up. "Jack, Jack!" he called out to me. "Can't do it!" I jumped off the train and tumbled back onto the gravel of the yard. Bill finally made it up to me, swayed dramatically, and then crumpled to his knees. We did that 'til about two o'clock in the morning, for train after train.

The leaving trains were getting scarcer so I took to grabbing Bill by the collar and the back of his pants and running him up to the train. The idea was to throw him aboard and then jump after him, but we either got our legs tangled and the two of us just collapsed into a dusty heap while the train pulled away triumphantly, or otherwise I mistimed the throw and ended up tossing him against the side of the train car rather than through the gaping open door of one. Then he'd bounce off, seeing stars, and fall into me, arms and legs akimbo. So that's why Bill was on his back, explaining the metaphysics of Neal's kidnapping and Cthulhoid physiology to me. The concussions of enlightenment, there's nothing like them in the world anymore. I threw Bill up against another hulking turtle of a train car, but by dawn he wasn't getting any smarter. "Good Neal, or evil Neal? Which one are you even trying to save…or to destroy? There's a battle in each of us, you know. Reason versus madness, base matter and dreamy illusion, perception and memory. He's transcended the real now, you know. We can't go to New York to save Neal, for he is all around us, sitting naked on our forks with every bite of meat…." Eventually he nodded off.

The flats heated up quickly under the sun. We hid under a tarp as the few night shift guards sauntered out and were replaced by an army of foremen, Pinkertoon goons (real goons with black pebble eyes and arms as long as apes') and freight haulers. I briefly considered sauntering on up to a gang of workers and blending in, then hopping a freight, but I was sporting a few too many bruises for that, and Bill had even more, plus his wrinkled pimp suit. "Just act natural," I could tell him, and I knew he'd blow our cover in a minute with some obnoxious rant or mouthful of vomit landing on the wrong goose-stepping boot.

It was Neal who found us. Some thug of a man, more fireplug than primate, shuffled up to our hiding place backwards, and on the back of his head was Neal's face. The worker's hand ducked behind his back and wiggled its fingers at us, like a television maître d' looking for a few bucks in exchange for a decent table. I made to move but Bill put a hand on my shoulder. "You're still a mark for that character, you know? You don't know whether this mugwump might lead you—right to the slaughterhouse as likely as anything. Are you ready to be Vienna Beef, eh? The mark inside is the mark you can't beat, Jack. Neal knows it, now the damn mugwumps know it."

"We can stay here 'til we get caught by someone who doesn't even pretend to be friendly," I reasoned. Then I laughed out loud. It was horrible. Bill and I were every movie serial hero and sidekick. "It's a trap!" some underfed faggot actor cries (his voice cracks professionally, so the rubes who paid their two bits for a picture show will think he's a kid), but the square-jawed protagonist can only squint into the distance and declare, "That's a chance I have to take." Cut to titles, then on to the newsreel. Denver is now the West Coast, millions lost beyond the sea, their souls imprisoned on old R'lyeh. Sounds like something Neal would crib for his book. So I went and Bill followed, muttering and wiping dust from his knees. Was this the feature, or just the cartoon?

We were led to a distant corner of the yard, Neal's plaintive face stamped into the hair of the shuffling fellow we followed. He brought us to a funnel flow tank car, the sort of thing you might use to transport kaolin clay slurry, molten sulfur or the horrid ichor of the earth's very bowels, and in his weird backwards way gestured for us to climb and see if we couldn't squeeze in through the top valves.

Even if the car were empty now (Bill rapped on the side of it experimentally, but didn't come to any conclusions) it could be filled at any stop. We'd be alone in the dark, huddled together, probably bruised and battered from rolling around all over the slanted belly of the tank, when corn syrup or even hot asphalt pours in. We might not even be awake for it. But Neal, oh Neal… I looked at what I could see of his eyes, which weren't much as they were just molded hair on the back of some mugwump head. Would he really betray me so utterly? Wanderlust is what led him to dump me down in Mexico years ago; he ran off, following women and his muse while I broiled alive with a fever on a stained cot. And from that expression, even obscured by the media of skull and hair, I knew this was the real deal Neal, not just some haunted chimerstry. But, he did drive off and leave Nelson to die, when was it—a week ago? two?

I left him to die too, didn't I? I hadn't even thought about him since then, and now he's not just dead, he's deep under the burgeoning Pacific in Cthulhu's dark embrace. Trust this Neal doppelganger; damn, I was barely sure I was human myself at that moment. Luckily, in the next moment, a growling pickup truck pulled up and idled. Bill rushed up to it and grabbed the driver by the ears and started yanking, while I grabbed the body. Neal's face shimmered and shifted into a horrible tusked boar, but I kept low as a barbed prehensile tongue spilled forth from the boar head. The human slab of man was belching for help too, and trying to jerk free, but I kept low, wrapped my arms around his thick waist and finally threw him onto the ground. I jumped over the tangling whip of a tongue and ran to the truck.

Bill hadn't gotten the driver out, but managed to shove himself in through the open window. His legs were sticking out and flailing like he was trying to swim for it. I rushed up to the door, opened it and helped pull the driver out, then slid into the driver's seat, yanked Bill over my lap and dumped him, crumpled and upside down, into the passenger seat and punched it. We were off in a roar of dust, whooping and shouting and flipping the old bird to the backwards boar-faced thug and the chump we just rolled for the ride.

We blasted over the border and through the steel tentacle buildings of black Gary, Indiana. Bill stayed twisted like the letter C, but upside down and backwards, till we had hit the heartland, then finally snaked into seat properly. "Look, a farm," he said, nudging me with his elbow. The highway was a knife's cut through endless fields of blasted grain, sprinkled with skeletal cows. Only Bill Burroughs could look out at that landscape and see a farm. I saw poisoned earth and chewing machines swaying in the air-warped heat. The silent, sleepy, staring houses far from the roadside could tell all that had transpired here in these late days, but they were not communicative, being loath to shake off the drowsiness that helped them forget. It would have been merciful to cut the wheel hard and drive right up to the front stoop, and to throw a flaming thatch of blackened wheat through the window, to kill these houses, to end their haunted dreams. But Bill nudged me again and smiled and said, "Look, a farm." It wasn't getting any funnier, not the next twelve times he said it either. "Look, Dachau," he should have said. "Look, the moldy tainted heart of our heartland. The nation's breadbasket with a clicking mandibled-chin head in it rather than a sweet loaf," he should have said.

"Look, a farm," again. Then, "I need to take a fucking leak. And we need gas too."

There were rest stops on the highway, but on this fatal plain we had to be careful. Slow down when we see one on the highway, try to spy with my little third eye the taint of extradimensional evil, but then it may already be too late. Grease monkeys swarming on our car, smashing the windows with tire irons, dragging us into the local diner for deep frying. So no, you don't slow down at the first truck stop you see, that's where they are waiting.

But you don't just zip past it either, not when your pickup is already coughing out black exhaust. The beetlemen behind the counters or a pear-shaped goblin waitress peeking through the venetian blinds in a little side window spot you half-dead on the road, acting all casual, and call ahead to the next rest stop. Pull in there, fast or slow, and they're waiting for you. All smiles, all lips twisted and hardened into thick chitinous hooks. All service too. Sure, fill the tank, have a cup of joe (on the house even) with two lumps of sugar, one for the coffee and one for the gas tank. Then, three miles down the road, when the truck wheezes and fails just over the horizon, we come for you, drag you out of the cab, slice your vocal cords and listen and laugh as we drag you over the hot asphalt back not to their stop but to the one before. What's left of Jack and Bill, bloody and stained roadkill, served up as Sunday hash in two different diners.

Maybe the third stop, if you have enough gas because you sure as hell don't want to be walking the shoulder alone with nothing but an empty gas can, if this purloined jalopy even has a gas can, because you won't even be able to throw a punch before they get you. And at that third rest stop you don't slow down, you blaze on in, tires squealing and red hot. You grab the gas quick, at gunpoint if you have to, if guns even work on these shambling monsters, and shove a wedge of apple pie in your mouth, roll out on the bill and hit the road before the cops or great tentacles made of bright noonday sky itself come to claim your soul.

"There's a rest stop," Bill said. I slowed down and pulled in without incident, and haggled for some gas. The gas man was a good old boy who'd seen better days. He had a Bible in one hand, a whittling knife in the other, and was just leaning and looking, his eyes little pebbles. I walked right up to him and told him that I'd stolen the car, that I was a great horrible beatnik and that if I didn't get to New York and soon like, the stars would align and the world would be consumed by great Cthulhu, or maybe just destroyed by Azathoth.

"Have you been washed in the blood of the lamb?" he asked. "Have you been slain in the spirit?"

"Sure." What else can you say to that? And there was that one time when a hobo preacher laid hands on me and I whooped it up for nearly an hour, in the grasp of some golden fist, though that could have been a parlor trick. I meditated for days after, searching for that elusive clump of nerves or spiritual door that would make it happen again, but I never found it, except in the tickytack of the Underwood. Anyway, we really needed gas and the fellow liked Bill's watch, so we filled the tank and two five-gallon tanks we found in the back of the truck, plus a redneck blessing written into the dust on our hood with his finger.

I pushed the truck hard and it ate highway like a rattling monster. The steering column was a thing of primitive beauty, a divining rod. *Ease up now, then punch the gas hard, Jack*, it told me with faithful vibrations. We skirted the edge of the performance envelope, goading the engine on with pumping splashes of hot gas and then easing up just before something might start to smoke. The last I wanted was to crack the head in Indiana and wait on the road for the cult of Cthulhu to skin us alive, or for that matter, for the goddamn Pacific Ocean to show up. The jalopy loved me though; like the sweetest girl it guided my hands to the sweet spots and we drove on with a fierce energy. Bill slept, head cocked to the side like a dead man, a string of drool writing spirals on his lapels.

Indiana was gone by the time I had to pull over and pour one of the emergency gas cans into the tank. The sun was high and a sunset red. The sky looked like orange juice; what Outsider Being had spilled his brunch mimosa on the terrarium dome of our sky? It was hot; I was probably going mad at about that point, but since Bill was such an old lady of a driver, I dared not wake him and have him take over. He would have stopped at every bathroom and corny roadside attraction on the way. Ancient genuine pointy rocks labeled 'Indian Arrow Head' under glass; skinned monkeys stuffed and displayed as stillborn freak babies; two-headed calves with heavy industrial staples glinting along the seam of the sinister head's neck. Who said America is in the grip of a weird evil *now*; we've always been fascinated with it ever since the first burly settlers chased sweet squaws into the woods, and came out smiling and dripping with sex and a bloody scalp. Even this Beat thing just led to what: a lot of bastard kids, bad poetry, and the junky faggot next to me who snored like he was percolating coffee in his sinuses.

Neal was still everywhere. Silvery Greyhound buses matched speeds with us and his face leered out in the flesh of tourist jowls from every window. He smiled, he commanded a hearty thumbs up from enslaved old men, he melted and attacked the bus driver, then tried to run me off the road, but my stolen truck could gun past an overstuffed bus any day. Other Neals waved from the roadside and left cans of gas and bags of little white pills; I filled up and munched them down by the handful. Eventually, my hands were shaking so much they vibrated through the steering wheel. I needed to switch off on the driving duties, quick like.

"Bill!" I tried to shake him but my fingers flowed like water through the fabric of his jacket and dribbled onto his shoulder. I turned back to the road just in time to see it cut hard to the left. I wrapped my arms around the wheel as best I could, my shirt and flesh splashed against my chest. We drove into the cliff face wall that bordered the highway and through it.

"It's a Stanley blade," the man named Gin said. He was a weird one, old Gin. Skull like a bird with eyes set so deep in his head he always looked scared and always scared me a bit, whenever he turned my way. Gin's thin fingers wrapped around the little knife and sliced through the newspaper headline. "And it cuts so easily, so well." He was English, his voice lilted. All his features lilted, the little bird man. Gin's hands, thick green and black tattoos spiraled and pointed their way up his well-veined arms. His shoulder rolled like a swimmer's when he moved.

Even his cut-up was like a ballet, beautiful to behold. Not much else was in this dusty room, dark and with yellowed newspapers stacked to the stamped-tin ceiling. Even the window was gray with dust and outside I saw a street corner like the black hoof of a great beast. I knew the rest of the town—though I didn't know what alien city it was supposed to be—would be rich with filthy bums and piggish slavers, married whores and deep black rivers stained from the crushed bones of the earth. What mountain of corpses was this built on? Indians, diluted and destroyed by hot firewater, stooped over Negroes toothless from sugar and beatings, or just plain old white folk huddled in the corner of their huts, hiding from the leaping shadows and dance of firelight? Taxman was always coming, pulling behind him his cart of war....

I looked up and smiled at the applause. "Pulling his cart of war," I repeated and nodded, because that's what intellectuals do even when the clappers are just stooped-over roaches with out-of-fashion hats balanced on their heads, and a few slick trained seals in the cheap seats by the kitchen. I looked down at my notes and saw only the jibberish of dreams. "Or just on the road," I read, squinting, trying to fool the letters into coherence. "Carrying garden tools for no good reason to anyone but Neal, looking to get back to Denver or New York. I nearly cried at the thought of missing him, and bit my lip hard, 'til my mouth filled with tired blood in the game." They applauded anyway, the way Auntie applauds her Mongoloid neighbor boy for singing 'Happy Birthday' wrong.

"Off to he who called himself Doc. Bury a body in the desert, or dig a tunnel to a sweet freedom underground and away from the blasphemous sky. Neal announced who he was to a wall, and shoved an old feller, extinguished, thin, and named Howie at me, foreign cigarettes on me and Howie smiled and chest until I showed off a gap them what they wanted."

After. Or waiting for my show to begin. At the bar. With a drink. Tasted like broken glass, like warm ice that won't melt. Tentacles, flippers, hot human hands patting my back as if to say "Better luck next time, chump." Once after drinking sixty great rounds in 1942 I found myself wrapped around a porcelain toilet, vomiting so hard that I didn't just stain the bowl, I chipped it. I spit up my soul and stayed tied to the commode like a dead vine while three days and nights of winos and sailors did their business over, around, and on me until I was entirely encased. I could have stayed there 'til this day and just woke up this morning and walked into a whole new world that had already passed me by. Then I'd expect someone to walk up to me in shimmering space armor or a Mao jumpsuit and tell me, "Better luck next time, chump." Not today though, not when I was in *The New York Times*, not when I had the word visionary stapled to my name like a second head. Something from my drink was sharp against my tongue. I reached into my mouth and pulled out the swift triangle of a Stanley blade. I put the point to my wrist and cut, up....

"Aigh!" Bill cried out, throwing his hands and elbows up into his face, "I can't stand this goddamn car." I lolled my head and lifted one eyelid. The yellow road lines were drifting into the view of my window on the passenger side. Quite a trick. Bill was a better driver than I thought, going sideways and all.

A million Greek relatives spun in lazy snake circles, out the door of the VFW and then back in to the hoots and gasps of the few white friends Memere invited. Stella was radiant but I really wanted to marry the puddle of sticky whiskey at the bottom of my glass. Bouzouki music trilled endlessly under stomping and applause and tinkling glasses and forks. I looked down, my rented lapels were out to here; I could have flown off and escaped if I had a running start out in the parking lot. The purple tentacles in my salad writhed suggestively to me, but I couldn't find the proper fork to stab them with. I never wanted a formal wedding, too square even if the dances were all group rounds. I could die right here, hand my soul to Stella and have her eat it with the cake. She had a tv, she had some money, she had a couch. I'd be fine. *Just leave me alone,* I'll tell her five days a week, and two days a week I'll lay her and that will keep her quiet and purring, so I can die in the living room, a moment at a time, like I want to.

Gin poked me hard and got my full attention. His hand wasn't in front of my face, it was somewhere in the inside of my face, his fingers in my eyes and nose like they were the triple holes of a bowling ball. I could still see though, see those deep-set coal eyes demanding my whole world from me. "The cut-up is a random event, but that doesn't mean you have to accept any snowflake lattice of word and image, Jack. You're still in the driver's seat, you and Bill together. Remember what Neal did to your old immortal town of Denver; he tore it apart right in front of you. So are the beings from beyond—he's nothing but the teeniest phalange of their might and chaos, a finger dragged along the dust of an antique market." He pushed the knife into my hand and nodded towards the newspapers. "Cut again."

The clicking of the blinker woke me again for a moment. "How long have you been trying to turn?" I muttered to Bill, who explained that the road was a spiral sinking away from the surface of the planet and that it was only headed in one direction. Down. He'd been making a left-hand turn for hour after hour. Our land was being torn apart, its remains washed away in a rain of black spirits from the darkening sky. Reputation aside, I never traveled directly from end to end of this great country—there were always false starts at rainy bus stops, big times missed thanks to some cotton picking adventure, or a premature end to my journeys thanks to fistfights and fevers. My trip through the American Dream was never made in a bee-line, how could it be?

Marie's secret enlightenment, her last-minute whisperings, saved me again. Do the absurd thing. I looked in the glove box and found an AAA map in folded tatters. I tore the pieces apart and shuffled them atop the dash. Bill didn't even look at me, he was leaning over the steering wheel like The Red Baron in his Fokker. I built Ohio and Pennsylvania a new system of veiny highways, and I cheated. I threw half the map out the window, extinguishing hundreds of miles; it would have been bad news for thousands of ordinary folks if they weren't all mugwump slaves already.

"Make the next right, Old Bull," I told Bill, and suddenly, like a spotlight on a dark stage making that golden saxophone shine, there was a right turn to be made. We hit the turnpikes in Pennsylvania and Jersey and I paid the tolls in bewildering haiku. My *kireji* shocked the poor late-night bastards. "Earth burns, becomes smoke," I told them, then I said a secret line that explained it all. I don't remember those seven syllables to this day, but it beat trying to pay with tainted change. One toll booth operator looked like a mandibled Neal but old Bill just screamed like a woman, floored it and blew right through the gate, taking the yellow and black beestriped guard arm with us for half a mile after. "How ya like that, you goddamn sumnabitch! This is my fucking world, and I'll stomp my feet wherever I like, over and through every magic circle your Wall Street wizards make! Notional boundaries, conceptual traps, I'm destroying all rational thought, and taking your ugly shit stalls with me!" The next booth, this one also holding a Neal doppelganger, Bill just rammed right into over and over, and when it collapsed we drove over it. "Now that, my friend," I howled, "is the spirit!"

That was a fine truck we stole.

I drew new highways in the blood from my well-chewed fingernails on the glove box's map and scraped a free road from central Pennsylvania and parallel the Jersey Turnpike. No man's cosmic enthusiasm could endure that labyrinthine road, but the force of Buddha's palm guided us along a new path. It steadied our backs. Up through the pine barrens, past the flaming chemical plants that really burned earth into poison smoke (and made us beg, each and every day, for more plastic marvels, more disposable moments, more dead tv dinners), and into the squalid Negro cities. By dawn, we were in Hoboken, where the air smelled of factory coffee from Maxwell's down on the far end of Washington Street.

We switched off again and drove us through the mile square city. The dregs of society lived here; Negroes were but shadows and the poor whites starving Dachau ghosts. The bars never closed in Hoboken; I could taste beer on my tongue with every breath. Morning ferries were pulling out, loaded high with miserable drunks trudging back to Manhattan—they came here at two when their bars closed and stayed 'til dawn, then shuffled to Charon's own barges. Back to their newsstand kiosks to hawk disaster for two bits. To Bowery factories, to slap together industrial ovens. Floors needed sweeping, shirts needed stitching. You want a night sweeter than wine, you pay for it in the morning, with a hangover, a stiff workaday shift, and a little chunk of soul carved right out of you with a sharp Stanley knife.

But across the river, topping the brown Hudson like a crown, was Manhattan. Buildings stretched to the heavens, whose brothers the mountains are. It was not like any city on earth, for above purple mists rose towers, spires and pyramids which one may only dream of in opiate lands beyond the Oxus. Majestic above its waters, its incredible peaks rising flowerlike and delicate from pools of mist to play with the flaming clouds and last stars of morning.

But threaded through this beauty were the dark tentacles of great Cthulhu. He had beaten us home, the prize was in his grasp already. The heart of the world, concrete and fleshy, green money blood pouring in and out from every corner of earth though arteries of commerce and culture, all but choked up and poisoned with the madness of dead gods' dreams. I wanted closure, I wanted to walk on the water and run howling through my old streets, looking for the last big time but instead all my senses screamed a single word—*Horror!*—an oppression which threatened to master, paralyze, and annihilate me.

Bill parallel-parked badly and rubbed his eyes. He left the truck behind without a word and followed his nose to some hash browns and scrapple. Turning away from the skyline I remembered I was hungry for breakfast too, and followed Bill into the diner.

Chapter Eleven

Hoboken is the pus-filled appendix of Manhattan, a crushed city of filthy puddles and horrible caramelized smells (coffee in the mornings, Tootsie Rolls afternoons when the factory starts up). Nobody lives here, everyone is on pure survival mode. Even the little Puerto Rican girls who jump rope two at a time give you the ol' slit-eye as you walk past them. Horrible people, all of them. When I followed Bill into the diner it was just in time to see the waiters hustle and push the tables around a screaming hulk of a man with a head like a cinderblock. From behind the counter the fry cook, howling to himself in some ululating language, jumped into the ring of tables and put up his dukes. They started circling each other seriously, both calm except for the shouting, bobbing and rolling their fists in slow motion.

The fry cook wasn't five and a half feet tall, and Squarehead was more like seven, but the big man took the little bantamweight seriously. The cook swung hard to the body and got inside Squarehead, peppering his stomach and ribs with rock-hard rockets—he was a little guy but his arms were like suspension bridge cables. Squarehead raged and swung his huge oak arms but the little guy squeezed in right up against his brick wall of a torso and started laying in heavy shots, backing the big man up against the edge of one of the tables. Cookie must have been a club fighter and a good one, but he was too confident and ate one of Sqaurehead's chaotic haymakers. A waiter waltzed up behind the barricade, pulled out a blackjack and smacked Squarehead right on the top of the head with it, and when he didn't immediately go down, started drumming him down, each blow taking an inch or two off Squarehead's height 'til the crazed giant reached his knees and then keeled over at the fry cook's feet. He shouted again in curlicue language (Greek, Italian?) and the waiters and busboys quickly shifted the tables back to their old positions on the dusty floor, then picked up Squarehead (it took all five of them to get his carcass into the air) and tossed him out into the street. Bill and I were the only customers in there and the way the fry cook was looking at us as he resumed his place behind the counter didn't make me want to insult him by backing out and looking for some other greasy spoon, so we walked up to the counter, Bill's hat in his hands, and took a seat. The old cook licked the pink right off his split knuckles and nodded. "So, my friends," he asked over the squealing of heavy tables being dragged back into place, "what will it be?" as friendly as all get out, except that he'd probably call the man who raped his daughter "my friend" too before pounding him into a meat sauce.

I had the spaghetti with meat sauce and loved it. I loved it like I loved Hoboken and all these slimy little lives in the shadow of the haunted skyscrapers across the gray river. At least they were human! Even Squarehead, even the Negro who relieved himself against the balding tires of our truck, even the squinty-eyed Mongoloid kids who chewed lead like candy never sold their souls for some dubious starry wisdom. Death filled the spoiled air in Hoboken, but it was a natural death, the death of attachment, the death of fill-in-the-blank. I could feel a balloon over my head, tethered to my own mortality, whenever I turned to the east and saw the city on the opposite shore. We spent a week in Hoboken, plotting. Gathering intelligence.

We held court every night in the diner, after spending our days wandering the few streets here to find our fellows. The beatniks had already been chased out of the West Village, their apartments torn to shreds by bankers driven insane by Cthulhu-tainted money. Some had been to the city, wading through the dark and flooded Hudson tubes—the trains stopped running weeks ago. Others took rafts at dawn and paddled across the Hudson to see what was what, or chugged up north then walked across the George Washington Bridge.

"We're invisible," a girl with kohl-stained eyes told me over tea and reefer. "Like a hand in a beehive, if you don't bother them, they don't notice you. Not these mad mindless cultists. They walk the streets in robes, ten abreast." She didn't smile, it was like those muscles had been pulled from her face. She wouldn't smile if you tickled her feet or hugged her tight and told you you loved her. She wouldn't smile if you meant it.

"There are mundanes too—you'll see them when you go ashore. They sit by their windows, an eye peeking out between the ribbons of their blinds, waiting for their world to return." She took a long drag and then said wistfully, "I wonder if anyone has starved to death yet. Cats eat their dead owners, you know. They only wait a few hours to do it. With a dog, they'll sit there and watch a corpse, whimpering and waiting to be fed. Cats get hungry."

This girl was a serious head. I just now noticed that for as good-looking as she was (ironed hair, dainty nose, sweet round chin), near everyone else in the room had given her five feet of leeway in every direction. They crowded in the corner to talk to Bill, or hung out by the door.

"Are you a cat or a dog, old Jack?" she asked me and before I could give her a witty answer, she cocked her head, peered at me with those black and rounded eyes and said, "You're a cat person. That's good, I don't want to get too attached to someone who is going to die soon." She leaned forward, took the back of my head in the palm of her hand and kissed me like a man would. Heck, she kissed me like I kissed so many girls with her haircut and a tenth of her brain. We spent the night together in some moth-eaten sleeping bag in a broom closet while Bill did the brain work with the gang outside. Just as well, my heart wasn't in this adventure anymore.

In the morning after the kohl-eyed girl skulked off looking like a raccoon, I poured a cup of coffee (Where was I? Some artist's loft? Everyone else had split anyway) and stepped outside onto the roof and saw Manhattan again. I poured the coffee out (caffeine is a drug—I needed to be utterly straight) and settled down onto the tar beach to meditate so that I might peer beyond the purple veil of haunted smog that rested over the island like a shawl on some withered old lady's shoulders.

In the reflection of the new glass and steel buildings, in the shadow of old baroque bones, I saw it. The *deus ex machina.* Manhattan was it, the God of the machine, pumping out horror after horror. Every postmark on stamps meant for Big Sur, all the lucky train cars and sloshing tanks of gas, all to drag me across the country without just giving up to the drunk or to the sweaty arms of some girl (I could still smell the kohl-eyed one on me, on my neck and fingers, she was unripe like a March peach). Cross-country travel wasn't even that hard, really. Neal was there to tear up the landscape in Denver, sweet and convenient beer there to deaden my senses from the madness of the skies in Kansas. We kicked through challenges like bathroom doors but it was all thanks to *deus ex machina*; the unexpected yank of a lever, the dark man with his gun, the party gone on just a minute too long.

Another realization in a month of realizations: it needed me. Whatever it was, whatever sinister force was the real Prime Mover of all this clockwork grue (Cthulhu, the shoggoths, they were mere shadows on the wall of this cave, I knew), to the almighty It, little *ti jean* had cosmic significance. Have enlightenment, will travel.

I struggled to detach myself from the marionette strings of self, to dance free and off the beaten path, but it lead me right back to my buzzing morning thoughts. Was it September yet? It was warm, but not so hot as summer. Rivers had a cooling effect on nearby land, like bodhisattva's smile on a crowded battlefield. The cuts grew kinder. I found myself wishing for my Underwood so I could write Neal a letter about all these crazy times, the realization between syllables of haiku, but then I remembered that he probably knew all this stuff already. He always lived life on a string, but he was no holy fool; Neal Cassady was a cosmic dupe.

The systems for planning always fail. Everything, anything, we all fall to dust at the end of the day. That's why I never cared if any of my trips across the ribboned highway of America ever made it all the way; you can't succeed for failing anyway. Denver, Frisco, a hot couch in New Orleans, drippy automat New York, it's all the same, nothing but "Here I am!"

With a steel and concrete scraping, Maxwell's on Washington started up again. It didn't take five minutes for the smell of coffee grounds to sweep up the street like a hobo's blanket. I was agitated suddenly, up from half-lotus and pacing. Guns? Bug spray? The force of Buddha's palm? Caffeine was in the air and it tasted like war on my tongue and sweaty skin. The poetry of war, and me without a typewriter or even a chewed up pencil behind my ear. Bill was probably up now. He was always an early riser—a bizarre habit for a junky fag—I went to collect him so that together we could strike at the dark heart of America's nightmare.

The skinny Puerto Rican grinned and held out his bony Charon hand. The little outboard motor was already belching blue smoke, ready to push us hard across the river. We paid him with grass wrapped in butcher paper and he smiled and nodded. "Amigos, amigos! You're trusting men, strong boys I can tell. But I'm not coming back for you, I'm not going to wait for you either. If you get back, you get back on your own." He sat astern, opened the paper and starting running his finger through the weed, looking for seeds and stems, and didn't help us aboard. I jumped for it then held out a hand for Bill, who was weighed down by two huge containers of bug spray strapped to his back. We had that, I had a butcher knife tucked into my work boot with a spare sock wrapped around the blade, and I had woken up with a feeling that the stars were right. That's what we had. "And you swim the last twenty yards, I'm not going to moor either."

I swam in the Hudson once, back when the river was

still blue with tiny teardrop waves goading me on, back when even the fog was a warm embrace and leaves spilled from the parks of Washington Heights and floated under the docks. Even then as a stupid college kid I could feel my eyes burn whenever I dunked my head. Now the river was black and had an almost solid topography; our old Charon swung and moved the rudder to avoid hunks of steaming waste the size of couches.

And it wasn't the cult that did this, the filth here was all natural, all man. We had everything already, the altar had been laid out, sacrifices prepared. Charnel pits in Europe, hills of dead babies, bombs that could take this city of money changing temples out in a flash of light; the concrete and steel wouldn't even last long enough to crumble down to the ground. We're all so rich now that we're one step away from holding out the begging bowl and blinking away hungry flies. How could the elder gods resist such a morsel—we'd stuck the decorative toothpick in ourselves.

I turned back to look at Charon. He had a firm grip on the outboard's rudder and a deep smile. Bill sat across the bow, tilting forward to keep the cans from pulling him overboard and into the brown wake. "There is no way we can swim twenty feet in this filth, much less twenty yards. And we have the tanks to carry," I said. Bill said "Yeah. We have a better chance of hopping across the shitty little islands. This is like sailing through a goddamn rectum."

"That's right. So you're taking us to shore, or we'll just knock you right off your own motorboat and let you swim half a mile back to Jersey." Hoboken life was really starting to grow on me, or maybe it was the fecund stink of the world rotting around us. Charon laughed, one of those proud American laughs, and said "What an idea! I had the same." He pulled a pistol, a shiny little dame in a noir flick keeps me in her handbag number, right out of his pocket and leveled it at me. "You two, empty your pockets and jump. Better the river than the lead, no?" Bill shrugged out of one of the shoulder straps of his tanks and got the gun in his face instead, "No, you keep that. Just everything else you have. This isn't a cheap trip across the river—you can't take nothing else with you."

I didn't have a thing in my pockets and turned them inside out to show him, "We're just wandering fools, you know. Looking to save the world a bit?" Bill grunted, his face granite. "I'll drown with these things on." For a second I considered rushing the guy—maybe Bill was on the same wavelength. His junky body was tense suddenly, all the reserve morphine pooled up in his muscles had been burned out by adrenaline and fear. But he emptied his pockets with a futile defiance. He threw a worn wallet to the bottom of the boat, a tangle of string, a few soggy cigarettes, a bottle cap, a slim paperback from his jacket pocket, what looked like a chicken bone, and he reached into his pockets again before Charon, "All right, don't empty your trash out! Just jump!" He put the gun up to Bill's stone face. "Get your boyfriend to hug you. Two *maricons* together should be able to float."

I pushed him, with my brain. The boat, the gun, the river itself. Nothing came—the enlightenment well had run dry. No more miracles, just two sweaty and unimportant little men being poked at by a nasty little deathshead Puerto Rican. I so wanted to rush him but my limbs were heavy and Bill wasn't with me. He was on his feet, half-staggering. He slipped an arm around my waist almost too comfortably.

"Muchachos!" the ferryman said, "Listen, no hard feel-

ings? Better you take your chances now than face the terror ashore. They might just keep you alive forever, to see your faces when the world turns to dust beneath your feet. Swim to shore, then walk all the way up The Bronx. That's what I would do if I were you!" Then he kicked me square in the stomach, lightly really, but between Bill, the tanks and the rocking boat I lost my balance and fell headfirst into the drink. The bow of the motorboat loomed overhead as Charon cut hard to get back to Jersey, so we had to put our heads down into the foul water. It was like going headfirst down into a pile of compost, warm and viscous. Bill was a millstone around my waist, holding on tight like I was moored to something. My mouth was sealed, so vomit poured out of my nose and probably my ears as well, as the propeller ate through the water an inch from my face. We burst through the surface and gulped sweet city air. Bill spit up on my shoulder like a newborn and shrugged an arm out from under the shoulder strap of the bug spray cans. As he pulled away, our Charon waved at us, picnic-friendly.

We swam hard for shore. The river was against us, not the current, but the density. Swimming was like making snow angels in the drifts, and Bill could barely swim as it was. "Shit pudding!" he shouted. "This is nothing but shit pudding!" and then he vomited again through his nose because he was so busy yelling and carrying on with his cavern mouth and got it full of shit pudding.

I wanted to ask Bill to just dump the cans but my mouth wouldn't open for the stench, and it was so hard to even breathe with the heavy river wrapped around my chest. A big wave came and baptized us, slow and heavy. We fought back up to the surface, Bill suddenly stronger than I with his thick fingers wrapped right under my chin. He cursed like a moviehouse cartoon with every stroke, all rassin' frassin' umpin' jumpin' through lockjaw. I paddled after him, got one of the tanks up over the water, and eventually we hit silt and dragged ourselves up to the pier, a rotting wooden ladder, and finally under the eerily empty West Side Highway. We stood on cobblestoned West Street where it usually rained crashes and noise from above, where junkies and she-hes lurked by the pillars holding up the highway; but it was all empty, blank as pages.

"Wooo!" I shouted. I was covered in river slime and embraced it. "Better a filthy hog than a death cult bean counter any day, right Bill!" I danced around him—Old Bill was back on his knees, sighing and raking a shit-stained handkerchief over his shit-stained face—his teeth were blacker than usual. "Stand up!" I called out, and he said, "Shut up. I had to drag you through that muck. I'm going to vomit up everything I've eaten for the past month." He stretched out right in the middle of the street and turned onto his belly, and heaved a bit, one more comma in his long retch-intensive life.

I started walking, confident he'd pop up and follow me. I wanted to find a YMCA, spend six or seven hours in the steam bath, get some grub in me, and then reconnoiter. There were sure to be some friendlies around, in the old Beat hangouts, the old man bars, the libraries up at Columbia or down by Washington Square Park. Bill wasn't moving though, so I walked on back to him. He was unconscious in a puddle of brown muck. The streets were still quiet but there was no telling when a huge caterpillar the size of a train car would come rumbling down the street to claim him, or if a bacchanal of cultist insurance adjusters, teeth and nails red with the blood, would appear in a blast of screams and naked limbs to set Bill to rights with Accounts Payable. I looked around, found a small puddle of clear water between two broken cobblestones, cupped as much as I could into my hands and walked it over to pour it over Bill's mouth, then waited for him to recover his strength.

Chapter Twelve

It took us four starving days to find anyone left with a soul. Most of Manhattan seemed utterly deserted and the ripe smell of recent death hung on entire blocks. Like they had said back in Jersey, we'd sometimes catch a yellowed eye peering out from between curtains or a weak and shaking hand quickly pulling down a blind, but people had either evacuated the city or were right behind us and would duck, a hundred thousand at a time, behind one lamppost whenever Bill or I turned to look over our shoulders. The Y on 23rd Street was abandoned, but the water ran, so we could drink. We armed ourselves with bricks and went hunting for food, but most bakeries and butchershops we came across had already been looted. At night when the moon never came out, we'd hear the laughter of breaking glass and occasional howls of animal satisfaction. The red stars in the sky kept me from venturing outside. Bill found some toothpaste, and being faint, ate it all without sharing with me.

There weren't even any pigeons, or squirrels, or rats. The former two I would have eaten. I tore my thick right sock and made a sling of it and took to the streets at the crack of dawn, the lone hunter. The sling would do no good if I ran into any cultists, or any horrible clicking beetlemen or great beasts too horrible to describe, but I was ready for any squirrel the good Lord might send my way. There was nothing for me, and no food in any stores and not even a trail of ants on the sidewalks to follow to a spilled ice cream cone or piece of bubblegum. Leaves curled up all black on the trees, never flaming into autumn or falling. The morning searches made me hungrier too, and my belly growled in inchoate rage at me. I chewed on my fingers, eating little bits of my own salty skin, weak and humbled by mere waiting.

I kicked myself all the way back to the Y, so furious at myself I forgot to keep an ear out for the flap of wings in formation or for a roll left unscavenged from an overturned bread truck. Four days with no food was a cinch. Kids in China did it all the time, and still grew up strong enough to march in place and shout out Red slogans on television. Women in Africa with babies on their withered breasts did it too, and made it to the relief station without so much as a swoon. Indians too did it, I'm sure, trapped on the reservations away from their ancestral hunting grounds. I let out a war whoop to be just like them. If I were an Indian with face paint and feathers I'd fit into this fatal city better. Anything but a plain old white man, demoralized and too clumsy to starve with honor.

Bill met me at crepuscular Washington Square Park that day. He'd had better luck. "I found a guy up in Hell's Kitchen manning a hot dog stand. There was no street traffic, and of course no cars that were still in one piece, but he was a wrinkled little man who told me that he'd been there for ten years and he wasn't about to stop now. 'The game's crooked, but I'm the only game in town now,' he said, and he laughed like a black lung miner."

"Did he want money? How did you pay him?"

"I filled out an I.O.U." He fished a grayish hot dog on a stale bun out of the pocket of his wrinkled suit jacket, all neatly wrapped in a paper napkin, and handed it me. "He wanted the top twenty five stories of the Chrysler Building, but I talked him down to the top seventeen. And after this all blows over, I have to spray his flat for free." I laughed at that, almost spilling my awful bite of frankfurter, but then stopped when Bill said, "He didn't want the first few floors because they're filled with human skin. All the bones from the bodies stacked up like bolts of fabric were pulled out of their eye sockets and assholes, he said. I double-checked his story. The vendor was mostly right."

"What was he wrong about?"

"I wouldn't call the first ten stories of a skyscraper a 'few,' " Bill said, casual as weather. "So, you ready yet, or do you need to digest?" I wasn't hungry anymore, but ate anyway and my wiener was gone in three bites. He nodded towards the south and we walked out of the park and down Thompson Street.

"What do you think those hot dogs were made out of?"

"Don't ask stupid questions, Jack."

Our determined tromping down to Wall Street to obliterate the Great Elder God who drowned California for appetizers and killed Manhattan as a sorbet stopped at Canal Street, because rather than the garish storefront signs with bold streaks of neon Chinese there was nothing but a wall of cold black flame rising from the yellow traffic lines. Bill just laughed and said "After you, Jackie!" ushering me towards the fire with the wand of his spray tank. I just ran east all the way to the Manhattan Bridge and back, huffing, to Bill. He shrugged and followed me at a more leisurely pace over to the west side. Even exotic Chinatown was abandoned, fish left to stink in the stalls, the ice having melted into slippery puddles already. The payphones still had little pagoda-style roofs, like altars lining the street, but there was nothing holy about that wall of black fire, fire that didn't cast a shadow on the sidewalks.

The flames sealed the street off from rivers East to Hudson, and neither of us was ready to jump back into the groaning and awful river, which had started bubbling with either life or boiling heat anyway. I tossed a traffic cone into the wall. It sailed right through and to the other side, making the local flames go translucent just long enough for us to see the frozen rubber shatter into a billion needle-thin shards.

"Under ground," said Bill.

"Under ground," said I, and we rushed to the nearest manhole and worked together to pull it up. The manhole cover came up easily, as it was already resting a bit off the lip. I rolled it to the side as Bill stuck his head down the manhole, stuck his arm down into the dark and lit his Zippo. "All clear!" he called out while picking himself back up; he ended up shouting "clear!" in my ear. I swung my legs over into the manhole and slid right down the ladder, landing with a neat splash. The tunnel stank, of course, but not any worse than topside, probably because toilets hadn't been flushed all that much for the past couple of weeks. All the rats were gone down here, too. Bill took the ladder carefully, holding on to the rungs with white knuckles and placing a shaky loafer down, then another, onto the same rung before moving down at all. The cans of bug spray were heavy, but he was really just mincing. We walked along the narrow ledge of the tunnel, not quite single file. We could have shared a jacket for all the room we had.

"So," Bill finally says after we walked a block or three in the dark that was more a silence of light than any real darkness. "If it is that easy to get around the firewall, why bother with it?"

"Well, the killers, the cultists, even the monsters, they have to travel too." Then I realized that we might not be alone in the tunnel and stopped coming up with clever ways to describe a dark hole and started paying attention for distant footfalls.

"No they don't. Whole towns can live in the area under Canal."

"Maybe it's not for us then. Sometimes it seems like the Elder Gods are fighting one another, or at least brushing up against one another and sparking huge waves of etheric lightning, just from that moment of stray contact. Is there a rival cult in Inwood or Harlem? Jets to Cthulhu's slimy Sharks?" Christ, I was so damn wordy that night.

"I bet some of these monstrosities can fly. Hell, Jack, you were able to erase seventy-five miles of interstate highway in your sleep. No, I think the flame is another thing entirely."

"What?"

"Landing lights. Cosmic runway. The cargo cult is asking for a palette full of baked beans and damnation." I was so hungry, I could smell the beans sizzling in their reddening tin can over fire and open air. They balanced so good on a pocketknife, baked beans did, salty and sweet at the same time, it was surely the cuisine of trickster gods. I slept so many peaceful nights with a full belly under moral stars, drifting off to the sound of some sage scraping the bottom of a can with the tip of his blade for that lucky blob of pork or a refugee bean. Manhattan, the center of the world maybe, but just a turd floating on the edge of America's great spirit. A melanoma maybe, or a wart to be lanced, to make way for more wandering poets and thick-fingered fur trappers. Anything but office work under buzzing lights and society parties held by celebrity couples with dead loins. My stomach shouted at me to pay attention to the tunnels, to listen for chants and distant screams. Bill was still going on about something, though.

"We didn't see anything like them from the boat last week. Those flames are new, spewing out god-knows-what kind of radiation that only three-lobed burning eyes can see." He looked at me, Zippo right under his chin, to cast his face in Bela Lugosi shadows. "The stars are right," he intoned, right from the bottom of his register. "This is the night for a proper sacrifice. But are we in time to stop the ritual and save the world, or are we just pawns sliding our way to a fatal black square?"

I had just enough and lost my bodhisattva grace right that second. I shoved Bill hard up against the sloping sewer wall and grinned at the ringing of his skull meeting pipe. "Bill!" I shouted, and winced, half-expecting an eruption of rat squeals and scampering that never came. I just heard myself, a tinny AM radio echo bouncing down the labyrinth. "I am going to bash your goddamn skull in! I cannot take another minute of this warped and filthy planet! How many people drowned in California, how many skins did you count up this morning without shedding a single tear, you twisted junky piece of shit?" He opened his mouth, showing me his rotten little teeth, but I just clamped my hand over it and squeezed his cheek and jaw. "Not another word!" I barked, like a sergeant. My brain was just floating in blood and hunger; I could have chewed off and eaten strips of William Burroughs' pasty white face like fatty bacon right in the tunnel. It was getting to me, the death we had just missed but only saw hideous hand traces of. I wanted it real, hot blood in my face, the look of desperate struggle fading to shame and then dismembered peace. Then Bill twisted his arm, put the wand in my face, and gave me a blast with the bug spray. I screamed as the stuff burned through my eyes and filled my sinuses and hit something hard with the back of my head. I think it was the planet Earth.

Long fingers prodded me awake. Neal's. Not from Neal's writerly hands, the thin fingers that were too fine for honest work but just excellent for writing letters that went down like tubes of bennies and for getting locks to open. The fingers on this Neal were longer, like drumsticks tipped with pointed nails. He was the same otherwise, except distant, as if I were staring at him through the bottom of a glass.

"You're here," he whispered. "Finally, ol' Jack Kerouac has found me. The cult has changed me. Baked my bones and rolled them thin, my skin is like baked potato now. Be gentle, gentle." He picked me up off the ground, gently. I wasn't sure if he was addressing me or just talking to himself like a person who has finally and utterly lost his mind. I didn't feel too good, I could feel bruises everywhere. We were in a little room, still in the sewer, and some blue night sky light was spilling through a sewer grating a few feet over our heads.

I moved to hug him and grunted as I stretched my arms, but Neal shrank back, slide-bouncing back like a marionette. "No no." I followed him as he drifted away, wiggling like bait. Around a corner and the walls around us fell away utterly. We were on a stone path twisting and spiraling towards some deep white light a mile or more below. Great bedrock walls, the very base of Manhattan, stood firm on my left as I jogged after Neal who oozed down the spiral like quicksilver. Heading down to the next lowest circle of hell, leaving Bill behind, following yet another doppelganger, it didn't make much sense, but I felt the pull of that light from far below. I wanted to saunter towards my destiny, to greet it with a lopsided smile and my hands in my pockets. The quiet desperation of the dead and the hidden topside in Manhattan frightened me more than torture and death.

It was a long trip down, like that last note from a trumpet. My legs ached but Neal's ophidian slipslide mesmerized me, like a snake charmer in reverse, so I moved on, the no-mind ignoring the pain of my calves and poor blistered feet. I didn't even blink when it began raining screaming beetles. They'd been crawling down the face of the bedrock, even over the toes of my boots, heading straight down the tunnel instead of taking the curves of the tunnel, but now they fell like rain, howling puny "Noooooos" and "Jeeeezzzuuuus" all the way.

I glanced up and saw Bill, a pale white dot, tromping down the spiral path himself, killing bugs all the way. Neal paid no mind to the hail of insects, but slid so easily over the path that none of their little bodies were crushed into juice until my boots got to them. I shed a tear for their screams but knew they would live again.

The world shifted within me; from down the spiral I suddenly felt that I was walking up towards the light, which spilled down onto me as I slouched towards it, sweating, hungry again, the hot dog long gone and this morning's breakfast of puddle water now stagnant and half-foul. Far below, Bill clanged and cursed his way behind us, carrying a Holocaust on his back.

A horrible, beautiful luminescence spilled forth from the entrance of the temple. A three-stoned arch, two pillars holding aloft a pitted marble lintel, beckoned to me. Neal slid in and I followed, feeling tingly and snowblind. It took a long moment for my eyes to adjust. The temple was whiter than an office; the light came from everywhere but buzzed like fluorescents. Desks filled the space, with enrobed beetlemen tapping away at thick slabs of adding machines in front of them. A mail cart rattled its way autonomously down the aisle between two rows of desks, and there was even a water cooler filled with a horrid yellow bile. And shuffling, so much shuffling and pushing of papers, into folders, then into the jewel-hinged jaws of gleaming file cabinets stacked five high (tentacles were handy for reaching up top). There wasn't a sound other than the rhythms of work, not even a lonely scream.

There was a great statue at the far end of the hall, though statue suggests a volition that the sculptor probably didn't have. It was a mass of impossible corners, crawling tentacles, hideous faces frozen in screams in relief over planes, abstract but feminine crazy-eight curves, forty feet high and twice as wide. It smiled like the Buddha.

The tapping was a counterpoint, a staccato disaster beneath the whirling dynamism of the crawling stone over temple walls. I felt it in me, like the thumps of a bus on a pitted road, my heart in the hands of mugwumps. The inevitability of destiny called me again, like when I walked the spiral, but I found a koan Marie left in a corner of my brain and asked myself what my face looked like before my ancestors were born. It was sufficient to defeat a bunch of adding machines, anyway.

"Behold!" Neal said, "the core of the cult! The stars are aright, Jack, only one thing yet remains." The beetlemen rose and from their robes pulled clubs of bleached bone to fondle. They shuffled across the drab business carpeting and stood in formation behind the still shimmering and shifting Neal, and presented a baker's dozen of evil scowls at me; their mandibles looked like obscene parodies of businessman smiles.

I laughed! Loud enough it echoed, probably all the way up the corkscrew spiral and to the dead surface world. It was an American laugh (I finally had one of my own). "Is this it? All that death, all these cosmic powers, and the temple of Cthulhu is a boiler-room accounting operation?" I giggled, like a girl, uncontrollable. Heeheeheeheeheeheeheeheeheehee. "This is ridiculous." Neal smiled too, a real smile. The mugwumps chattered and coughed up powder uncomfortably. One began slapping his bone against his palm, cop-style. In the distance, the *ping* of a carriage return sounded diligently.

"The world is an absurd place," Neal told me, his voice languid like old gin. "You know that, right? Of course you do. But it's dangerous too, problematic. Overdetermined. Everything causes everything, like a game of billiards with a million players going at once with their cues at a billion balls on an infinite field of velvet. Who can comprehend, much less protect, a dharma like that?" There were mutters of approval from the mugwumps. More slapping of bone and flesh too, in a stilted meter more Morse code than bebop. I would have been intimidated had my spirit not shifted two inches to the left of my body. The scene unfurled like a scratchy newsreel,

Neal's voice the bellow of an Edward R. Murrow or Weegee.

"We need you to join our little operation, Mister Kerouac. All this terror couldn't stoke half the haunted dreams we need to finally rend the veil between worlds, to let the starry wisdom of the Great Old Ones descend unfettered onto our fair cities. But you're a battery, a dynamo. Tying your shoes is an adventure; when Jack Kerouac finds a parking space, saints weep. Your soul can rewrite the world for us, just like a book. That's why you struggled across the country, squeezing out ghosts from your own past to push and prod you on, to make here. To be acquired by our concern." The beetlemen clicked with the forced glee of an office Christmas Party.

"I have kids now, Jack. Kids I love, and it's rough being a working man, being a drone before the queen. I need a book, a bestseller, an *On The Road* for the Age Of The Elder Gods. And you're going to be my main character!"

"Swell, Neal. That's real swell." The statue begin to shift and move, spreading over the blank white walls, casting snakey shadows everywhere. My grin was bigger than Christmas. Neal slid on up to me, his own smile wide too, the ends of his cheeks pinched into embryonic mandibles. "A book about two best friends. For years, they were best friends! Tilting at windmills, looking for love but finding only wet and smelly sex. Living the American Dream, masters of their fates while the drones who man the offices drive the nation into a dusty death. How's a book like that gonna end, Jack?"

"Well," I said, "when it was my book, it ended with you leaving me in Mexico with the runs."

Betrayal. The word hung in the air. Neal didn't quite

say it, but he and I and every mugwump in the room and probably the protean statue thought it all at once. So we were agreed. I hoped Bill would get here soon.

"Yes, yes," Neal said through deformed lips, his *esses* already sinking into a queer lisp. "Yeth. Betwayal." Distant echoes came closer and I smiled a little bit more. Between my feet frantic beetles flowed like streams, searching for a place to hide. Neal's jaw finally hardened into thick mandibles. If they were antlers, they'd be twenty-point numbers, the kind hunters would wait years to bag and spend a lifetime bragging about while bloating up with beer and venison jerky and finally dying in front of their grandchildren. Huge mandibles, open with pincers ready on either side of my face, the cover of a pulp magazine if only I were a curly-haired buxom girl threatened by the four-color Monster In The Mountaintop.

"Yeah Neal, but you betrayed me already. In my book. If you're doing your book, doesn't that I mean that I get to betray you?" I laughed again, "Wouldn't you betraying me again be a little, you know, derivative? Pulp fiction. I mean really, I saw it coming from a mile away. The top of the spiral, even."

The mugwumps slapped their bones into their palms as one, like savages calling for the hunt. Neal, the part of his face that was still Neal, his sweet eyes, stared at me so plaintive and wanting. "No, I'm not betraying you. I want you to come along with me, to the next great adventure. We explored this world already, conquered it, but there is a new one waiting to be born. A safe world, a world far away from frantic bourgeois thought. There's no need to search for God anymore, or to chase after enlightenment or race to the bottom of degradation just to see how it feels, to see if we're still human afterwards, because we'll know. The higher power. Join us. Join *me*, Jack! You can rewrite the universe, along with me!"

For that moment, I wanted to. I was getting old. I felt it all throughout this trip. The road I'd taken was already gone, and the moon I'd made so many girls under already blasted to powder by missiles. Even my dear party cities of Frisco and Denver were underwater, never to rise again, though R'lyeh rose a lifetime ago. Forms like dark shadows twisted against the walls, pushing like a newborn chick against its shell, in indescribable Moebius-strip ways. More tiny beetles crawled in, but twitched and died at my feet, sweet poison coating them like perfume.

Then I ducked, just as Neal's pincers snapped shut and took the top of my hairdo off. A hot stream of bug spray hit Neal and burned him horribly; his face went up in a howling smoke. The mugwumps converged on me, bone-cudgels raised high, but Bill was already among them, handling his wand like Doc Holliday, and one after one beetlemen fell, fell and collapsed into scatterings of beetles, the scuttlebugs bursting from their mouths and assholes. They fell easy, like drones do; the few Bill left standing I took down with quick rabbit punches and knee lifts, Jap-style.

Neal was up at us again, waving his arms, his cruel face zipping itself back into shape, human shape, as crunchy exoskeleton fell away smoking. He was standing still but still running at a hundred miles an hour. "Fellas, wait, you gotta understand. You don't see what's really going on! You're from the wrong side of the river on this one. I've been to the golden shore, and it really, truly is better this way. Destroy all rational thought, right? Well these blind gods have done that, with a greater understanding. You're not fighting me, you're clinging to mama's pussy lips and trying to shove your heads back into her warm little womb, get me?"

He went on, his speechifying hitting the intensity of Satchmo's scats. Bill didn't put much truck in with glossolalia though and raised the wand to spray Neal again, but got only an impotent little squirt. "Well, fuck," he said and a massive bedrock tentacle lashed out from the far end of the wall and smacked Bill to the ground like a rag doll.

The transformation of the temple was complete. The soothing (to the mugwumps) office setting crumbled like so much chickenwire and *papier mâché* and the gaudy horror of it all was revealed. The walls were made of stars and a billion fathoms of void. The statue was still huge, dominating the scene behind Neal, but it stretched off into infinity in two arbitrary directions, for it was *axis mundi*, the evil core of creation. The center of the universe waiting for collapse and heat death. Hungry for it. The cosmos itself was hungry for oblivion, the rush of stars and fruitful worlds spinning themselves to cinders and then spiraling down to a dusty death.

And there was Neal, and I. We weren't even standing on the smartly carpeted floor of the office temple anymore, instead we hung our legs over the pier of infinity.

"Behold," Neal said again, casual and smiling rather than dime-novel ominous.

"There's a quality to this oblivion that's a little unsettling," I admitted.

Neal nodded. "It's desirous. An evil desire. Here's a koan for you: What is the difference between having no desire and having desire for nothingness?"

"No. It's just that desire is what is evil."

We looked about the empty universe. "What do you

miss the most?" he asked me. And I told him. Everything. The smell of a girl's hair. My thumb, throbbing four hours after a wayward hammer smack. The chuckle after a good lay. Ham sandwiches. The hollow call of the bull-roarer over the outback. Keats. Pencil tips breaking in frustration and rage. Barbed-wire war. Even smug preachers fondling the leather of their family Bibles like it was a woman. I went on and on, pouring out everything I could remember about the world: The smell of beer. The nostalgic horror of a green plain seen through prison bars. Dead children, all bones and parchment skin, in India or old Hoboken. Soybeans spilling through gnarled fingers at market day. The first gold stamped into coins. Puffing Russians calling for nuclear holocaust as a matter of stubborn principle. It took forever to list everything I missed about the world, and there was still plenty of time left.

"Brains small, universe big." I wrote that down once in a notebook. My brain was too small to rebuild the world; I could barely do justice to the highway system and my friends. But there was something deeper in me, the divine spark Neal knew so many years ago, the one his kind face hoped to bring here, even as the dark lust for matter within him lured me to this same blasted corner of the cold infinite. I turned to him. He raised a finger and I was enlightened.

In every raindrop there is an ocean, and every salty ocean is a teardrop. I felt my mortality rise again, like a balloon, like it did in Hoboken as I watched man-animals pummel and betray one another for moldy bread and futility. Without that mortality, that self-imposed time limit, I could do it. My Buddha nature presented itself and the universe was reborn. Reordered. Beetles scurried back up an orderly bedrock spiral and into the mortal city to refill their skins and disentangle themselves from the stacks in the lobby of the Chrysler Building. Buddha gathered up moondust and pressed it like dough back into smiling silver. Oceans receded, Allen pulled himself up from the sewers and spit out gallons of sewage, able to breathe again.

I nearly gave it all away, but under the world I made, I saw the one Neal made: drowned coasts, the dead everywhere, clicking beetlemen working in their dark, satanic mills, illusions of gilded trade laid bare. Was it any less beautiful? Of course not—misery is mayfly, beauty dross. Only the spirit, ineffable, remains eternal. There was a choice though; I was given a coin and just had to flip it. And there was a choice for me too.

To be Buddha, to embrace bliss, and leave the world as I'd left it after my travels, in ruins. Or to cut loose the silver chord, to set the world alight by offering up my own divine spark, my chance for escape from suffering. Psychic suicide, that's what it was, nothing less. I'd pour every single joy I ever had into Creation, or it would collapse back into Neal's nightmare. Or I could wring myself dry like a dishrag, and walk the earth dead inside, the neighborhood dog-catcher or the blocked writer in front of an eternally blank and unspoiled page, without even the buzz of sweet Marie in my ear anymore.

What's the difference between having no desire and having desire for nothingness? Neal didn't know; that's why he threw his lot in with late-night poker games and cross-country chases for his own tail. He loved his own Nealness too much to lose it without wanting to take the rest of us with him. He desired nothingness, but thought he had no desire. How could the Dark Dreamer not awaken from his feverish sleep and embrace the poor boy? I wasn't too clear on the distinction between the two choices myself, really, but rational thought isn't the key to answering the irrational question, is it?

I offered up everything I was, all I could and ever would create, and swore never again to even glimpse the infinite. The world was born again, the stars all in their place, and as I separated dark from light, I pushed the dark down below the face of the deep.

Cthulhu wept, lost again to strange aeons. Office walls and windows returned, and the statue withered and died like December grapes. The mugwumps were gone, as were their robes, but Neal was there, standing before me, plain.

"Jack!" he said, his face experimentally trying out his old trickster smile. Then it faded. Neither of us had anything to say. He looked down at the carpet, awkward and confused. A breeze riled up some papers on the desk and sent them tumbling down. Neal's reform-school chicken scratch was all over them.

"Your book?"

"The first two thirds of it," he said. I glanced outside and saw that we were still in that bizarre null-space, the bit between a mad dreamer's eye spasms. It just looked dark really, like a moonless night. We heard a groan; Burroughs wasn't looking too good, but he was alive, conscious, his face a pomegranate bruise. I walked over to him and behind me Neal rushed after his papers. "Drop it," I barked, and he let some of the pages go, but about half were still crumpled in one nervous hand, hugged to his chest. I hoisted up Bill, and we began our long walk back to New York.

Epilogue

"Mah!" I called out. "Can I get another beer out here? And a little tuna fish sandwich, with mayonnaise?" It was Indian Summer in Northport, too hot to move. I was sweating so heavily that I was stuck to the couch. The tv buzzed at me, *I Love Lucy*. The grape-stomping episode in Italy. My own trip there was pretty neat, for a book tour, but I think I liked the black-and-white backdrop Lucille Ball danced around in front of better. Funny stuff. I swallowed the last gulp of beer and sucked fumes from my bottle, and called for Memere again, but she didn't answer. Probably napping upstairs. Or maybe she left to run some errands in town while I was dozing.

The main door was open so the latest troupe of Dharma Bums (this group actually had the t-shirts printed up with puffy letters and everything) ogled me for a bit through the screen door, which didn't keep the bugs out either. I threw the bottle at them, and it bounced off the distended belly of the screen, but they didn't leave. "I'll call the motherfucking cops if you don't go home right now, you fucking faggots!" That got 'em running, but they hooted and high-fived each other as they picked their way down the drive. *Jack talked to me!* they'd say later on back at Stony

Brook, and freshmen girls would unzip their pants like it was a magic word, open sez me!

I worked on my baseball scores for a bit too, in my notebook. Pictorial Review Jackson was getting on in years, and feeling every pitch in his shoulder and elbow. They cracked when he opened up a can of peanuts, his knuckles were thick and arthritic too. But I knew he had one more good season in him, and he smoked batter after batter in the Summer League. Jackson was going to go out on top. My pen ran out of ink, and when I shook it, it exploded just to show me that it had enough ink left to ruin two pages and dye my hand red. I couldn't very well wipe my hand on Memere's couch, so I carefully tore a piece of paper out of the back of the composition book (I hated to do it, as it usually makes the page on the opposite end of the spine fall out too, but what could I do), blotted as much ink as I could, then finally ripped myself up off the cushions and went to the bathroom to scrub my hands.

I came back, found a bottle of Jim Beam (the beer was all gone from the Frigidaire), changed the channel on the television set (I was right, Memere was gone. I hoped she was out getting a roasting chicken for dinner) and settled back down. It was getting dark so early these days, but it was too hot to enjoy. The news came on. More war stuff. Disgusting un-American hippies chanting with just enough power to keep us from really pushing into North Vietnam and handing those slants the thrashing they deserved. They were cruel little yellow things, they looked like bugs, even their women, crawling over the brush with near-featureless faces. And like roaches, they just kept coming out of the woodwork. Allen was on television too, embarrassing himself and me both. Faggot commie; I bet they wouldn't be so quick to stick him in front of the cameras if they knew how young his tastes ran.

There were so many different stories on the news that night, but in the end they were all the same. If the Negroes were rioting, it was because of the war when you got right down to it. They want all their rights now, just like white people, because we're fighting for freedom. Bodies were coming home, the chinks acting up, the Russian bear posing and growling. One of The Beatles farted again, that was news too.

Memere came home, but with hamsteaks and not chicken. I ate well though, and had a piece of bread after wiping my plate clean with it. I was going to go down to the bar and see what was up, but Memere asked me not to, so we had ice cream and watched the late movie together. Then she went to bed, and I flipped through the channels for a bit, then fell asleep on the couch.

In the morning I received a letter from Neal. He was fine, he said. He did that bus-driving thing and was going to be in another book, but still hadn't quite figured out the ending of his own *opus*. He had trouble with endings, he explained in twenty-five single-spaced pages, and I wrote "No kidding!" in the margins of page twenty-four. He didn't even end the letter really, his typewriter ribbon just gave out. Neal didn't seem to remember a thing; he just kept doing the same old stuff over and over. Make and impregnate a girl. Steal a car. Taunt the cops and then whine when he got busted or otherwise in trouble. Neal was a goldfish, forgetting his whole world every seven seconds and surprised to see his little plastic castle in the middle of the bowl. "All mine, all mine!" he says in the glub-glub voice of fishies, then he forgets he has a place to live again.

I went to Gunther's for a few drinks and brought my mail with me because I didn't want to talk to anyone, and keeping busy with a pencil and paper was a good way to get some space in this town, and a free beer or two from an admirer who just wants a peek at my pages. I got about a quarter of a buzz on, borrowed some change and went to the post office for stamps, but it was too close to the end of the day and they were out. I was outraged; how does a post office, even a Podunk little colonial set-up like my local, run out of stamps. It was ridiculous, but the hangdog man behind the counter could only say to come back tomorrow or to write my Congressman. Damn right I'll write my Congressman, and I'll have my stamps and hang-dog's job too.

I spotted some more fans milling about near the lawn, so doubled back and hid out at Jim's. Jim was a wonderful artist, he did tons of seascapes and looked like a pirate with his beard and broad shoulders. He had a chipped tooth too, and a scraggly beard, and plenty of gin. We split a tab of LSD and talked for most of the night about painting and jazz and *The New York Times*. I read the book section, but Jim couldn't stomach the op-ed pages. "Propaganda," he said, rolling his r's like the second-banana heavy in a spy movie. "Sinisterrrr prrrop-a-GAHN-duh!"

"I bet they drop the big one," Jim said.

"Never happen. One, there's no need for it. All we need is for everyone to show a little unity, to show some goddamn respect for this country, and we can get out of there by Christmas."

He laughed at me, cruelly. "Jack, those are *your* people, those kids out there on the street."

"Those little faggots have nothing to do with me. Anyone with a beret and a scarf can be a so-called bohemian these days. If they find something in my writing they can hang their commie theories on, that's not my fault."

"Sometimes it's like you're from a foreign country, Jack. A foreign time."

"All of life is a foreign country," I said.

I went home and ate leftover pasta in the light of the open refrigerator, right out of the bowl, with my fingers. The next morning I woke up with heartburn and just wanted to stay in bed but Memere was changing for laundry day so I had to get up. I caught the news at noon. "The war rages on…" the newscaster, some local square from the Hartford station across the sound said, but the film didn't show any raging at all, but just GIs smoking and draping themselves over Jeeps like they were cherubs snuggling up in fluffy clouds while Venus was born in the foam below. Their drug-dead stares said it all.

There was a knock at the door but I didn't answer it. Then he tried calling out to me, a yipping society poodle. "Jack! Jack! I drove out all the way from Oregon to meet you! Are you home, Jack? Are you in there? I'm going to leave something on your stoop, if that's all right. It's some poems, and a short story. Maybe if you have the chance you can read them and write to me, okay Jack?" Ol' who-ever-he-was rustled around in the bushes for a second, trying to peek in through the window, but he just yelped as he met the local shrubbery's thorns and ran off.

Some guru was on the television now, all smiles and a beard like gnarled roots. A sitar started up, high and teasing like the wave of a sly gypsy girl. It reminded me of something but I couldn't recall it. I was agitated enough to go back up to my room and dig though some of my Buddhist books. It was a koan, and a pretty good one.

The answer wasn't satisfying, but it was important, consolatory. I was mad for a little consolation. I read it aloud. "There were two wandering friends in China once," I said, addressing the rest of my bookshelf. "One of them was an excellent harpist, the other a great listener. When the first friend played songs about mountains shrouded in regal clouds, the second would say 'Wonderful! There is a mountain before us, we can climb to its peak.'

"When the first friend played about a fresh stream, the second would bow down low and exclaim, 'Ah, a stream! We can quench our thirsts with clear water!'

"But the second man, the listener, fell sick and died. The harpist cut his strings and swore never to play again. Cutting the string is the sign of the most intimate of friendships."

I had forgotten about that last bit. The phone rang and I ran downstairs to get it. It was my editor, calling about some paperback rights. We jawed for a bit, too, about city gossip; everyone was rushing around collecting money to take out full-page ads against some latest outrage, or in favor of it, whistling and erupting like roman candles burning bright exploding spiders in the sky, all to say "Look at me! Here I am, little world below!" *Pshew pshew*, burning up in the sky for you. All of it was just useless words. I was pretending to care, writing dialogue for Jack Duloz and mouthing it into a phone. I would have hung up on him, but I needed the money. My trunk full of old writing was running low, there was nothing more I could sell, nothing more I could pretend was new enough to care about.

The news was on again. I watched it on the couch while Memere read under her lamp. They showed the sweating jungle, leaves so green they bled into the blue sky, and someone off-camera talked about the possibility of dropping the big one. That would end the war but good, but what would the chinks do? What would Russia do? Fire their own missiles out of spite, wrap strings of smoke around the world like a bakery box and deliver us all, a care package destined to hell. That was the best they could think of, you know. Not today perhaps, but maybe tomorrow or in some other stumblebum conflict between freedom and misery.

Go ahead. Blow it all to hell. Crack the planet in half and let red magma pour out into limpid pools over the ruins. Deep underground, scientists say, the core of the earth is solid, because of the crushing pressure of the whole world wrapped around it. Like a rare black pearl in an oyster, it waits, shiny and smooth down to the last molecule, hoping for its time to float under the sun without the encumbrance of its old skin, of our little flea-bitten existences.

Let it happen I say. The world's been saved once, while every ungrateful son and daughter slept and dreamt their baseball and apple pie dreams. And all they can do when they wake up is raise the chant for death again. They miss their sleeping world so much. Good for them. Better to desire nothingness than to have no desire for anything, like me. I didn't even want the drinks; I just had them.

Memere looked up at me with worried eyes. I couldn't bring myself to smile at her. I excused myself and took a long bath with my notebook so I could figure out the Summer League's next set of games and scores.

The next morning I had to get up early, find the rake, pull it out of the garage, and clean up all the wind-blown pages on the lawn and branches that some jerk had left behind.